THE SYDNEY
ADVENTURES
CARAVANS
AND
CASTLES
WRITTEN BY 1 MARY WEEKS MILLARD

DayOne

© Day One Publications 2013

First printed 2013

ISBN 978-1-84625-364-5

All Scripture quotations are from the **New International Version** 1984
Copyright © 1973, 1978, 1984

Published by Day One Publications
Ryelands Road, Leominster, HR6 8NZ

TEL 01568 613 740 FAX 01568 611 473

email—sales@dayone.co.uk

UK web site—www.dayone.co.uk

USA web site—www.dayonebookstore.com

This book is entirely a work of fiction. Some actual place names have
been used, but the names of all people and the villages where they live
are entirely fictitious.

Printed by TJ International

Dedication

To Hannah, Joe and Becky, who are always
an inspiration to me

To Joanna,

with love & best wishes,

May Weeks Millard

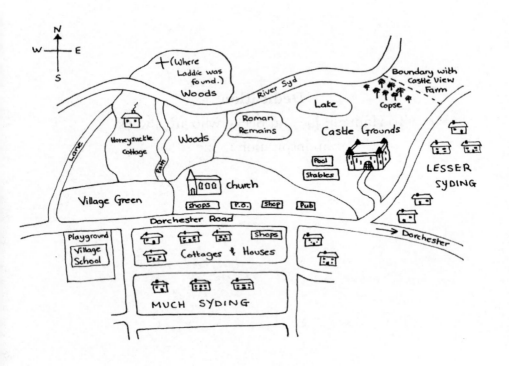

N
W + E
S

+ (Where Laddie was found.)
Woods

River Syd

Boundary with Castle View Farm

Copse

Woods

Roman Remains

Lake

Castle Grounds

Honeysuckle Cottage

Lane

Farm

Pool
Stables

LESSER SYDING

Church

Village Green

shops   P.O.   Shop   Pub

Dorchester Road

Playground
Village School

Cottages & Houses

Shops

→ Dorchester

MUCH SYDING

Map of Much Syding

Acknowledgements and thanks

My grateful thanks go to my ever patient husband, Malcolm, who graciously allows me to spend hours in the study and always encourages me. My thanks, too, go to Tirzah Jones, my editor Chris Jones and the team at DayOne Ministries. Thank you for having faith in me.

Chapter One

Mr Stevens, the teacher for years five and six was standing by the window. School had just finished for the day and his class had been dismissed. He noticed the first two children out of the gate, as usual, were Tyler and Theodore. Mr Stevens sighed deeply. He sensed that both boys were troubled, and he didn't know how to help them. He was a good teacher and cared about the welfare of his pupils. He had taught for many years in the village school of Much Syding; so long in fact, he had taught the parents of some of his present pupils! In all his time at the school he could not remember being so concerned about any of his pupils as he was about these two boys. He silently sent up a prayer that he might be able to understand and help them.

Tyler ran as fast as he could through the playground and out of the school gate. He looked both ways, crossing the road with care, and then went down a little path which led away from the village and into the woods. He didn't slow down until the school was out of sight. How he hated school! His dad and mum had hardly ever been to school and he didn't see why he had to attend. His mum kept telling him that things were different these days for the Romany people and he needed an education.

Once he was in the woods Tyler slowed down and began to whistle. He was always happy when he was outdoors. He felt so stupid in the classroom. It was hard just to sit still, especially on a lovely sunny day like today. He was almost eleven but still could not read very well. However, he knew all the names of the trees and wild flowers in the woods, and could follow animal tracks and recognise the birds by their songs! Hewas sure that nobody else in his class knew these things!

It took Tyler about twenty minutes to walk home. No one else from school lived near him; in fact, his family had no neighbours at all. They lived in an old cottage on the far side of the wood. Once it had been a game keeper's cottage, but his grandmother had bought it many years ago. Gran had realised that the travelling life of the Romany people was becoming more and more difficult and she wanted her daughter and son in law to have a house of their own. During the summer she still travelled in her 'vardo', the Romany name for a caravan, but in the winter she came back to the cottage. She was one of only a few remaining gypsies who still had a traditional painted horse-drawn vardo.

Tyler's parents had decided to live permanently in the cottage and give up the travelling way of life. They still owned a motor caravan which was parked near their home but they didn't use it very often. Tyler's father had found a job with the Forestry Commission managing the woods, and he loved it. He was glad to be able to work outside and it was he who had taught Tyler all about the plants and animals. His mother, like so many Romany women, was trained to be a fortune teller, but something had happened to her a few months ago, and now she had stopped doing that for a living; in fact the family's way of life had changed dramatically. Tyler was still very confused about it all. Up until that time they had been like all the other families in their clan, living and associating only with the Romany Gypsies, sometimes travelling, sometimes staying with others on big encampments. There had always been many cousins and friends to play with, and like all gypsy boys he had been learning to fight in the boxing ring. In their culture boys must be able to fight to defend their sisters; it was considered a very important skill.

But everything had changed since they moved to this house. They now only met up with the clan for important celebrations. His mother had tried to explain to him that they were Romany gypsies and were very proud of their heritage, but had become Christians and allegiance to Jesus came first and the clan second. Nearly all of Tyler's aunts and uncles, cousins and friends made fun of them and Tyler no longer knew where he really belonged. He certainly didn't belong with the 'gorger' children (as non-gypsies are called) at school. He wasn't like the New

Age travellers or the Irish travellers whom they met from time to time on traveller's sites and at fairs. Now he felt he wasn't like the rest of the Romany gypsies, either! Sometimes he felt very unhappy, even though at home he knew he was loved and wanted and he loved his parents and grandmother very much.

Three quarters of the way home Tyler sat down on a fallen tree trunk. He often stopped here; it was so quiet and peaceful. He heard the rustle of some leaves and looked up to see a squirrel running along the branch of a large beech tree; swinging from branch to branch. He marvelled at how agile the little creature was! Tyler knew that some of his uncles hunted them and the aunts made them into stew. He was so glad that his mum didn't do that because they were such beautiful creatures.

"How I wish I could see a red squirrel," Tyler thought to himself. His dad had told him how he had seen them when they were travelling, but they didn't seem to live in this part of the country. He knew the grey squirrels had driven all the red ones away by eating their food, but in spite of that, he still liked them! Maybe he could write about them for his homework; he had to write a story about an animal. He wished he could just tell a story, it would be so much easier! His dad made up wonderful stories and sometimes even wrote songs.

Tyler sighed. All his troubles seemed to have started when his dad and mum had written a new song. It was strange, he thought, that a song could change everyone's lives! He decided he must ask his parents more about that song. Why had they written it? So Tyler got up and ran the rest of the way home.

"Hi, Mum," he called, "I'm back!"

Chapter Two

*B*etty, his mum was waiting for him, sitting outside on the doorstep of the cottage, just like she used to sit on the steps of granny's vardo when she was a child. She gave Tyler a 'welcome home' smile and asked him how school had been. He shrugged his shoulders and answered; "OK. We had fish and chips for dinner; that was nice!" Tyler didn't want to upset his mum by telling her how much he hated it and how horrible some of the other children were to him. Romany children are used to putting on 'a brave face' when things are difficult and also used to being called names like 'dirty gypo', but it still hurt. In fact the Romanies are extremely clean people, more so than many 'gorgers' who criticize them.

They went into the cottage and Tyler looked around. He laughed out loud.

"Mum," he said, "You've gone and moved the furniture again!" His mother found it so hard to stay in one place; the travelling instinct was so strong in her that she moved the furniture around when she felt restless! Mum joined him and they laughed together until they almost cried!

She went to the kitchen and found Tyler a glass of delicious home-made lemonade and a biscuit and they sat out on the step together enjoying the sunshine.

"Can I ask you a question, Mum?" Tyler said.

"Of course, son," she answered, "Fire ahead."

"Why did you write that 'Jesus' song that changed you into a Christian and made us different from the other Romanies?" he asked.

Tyler's mother looked at her son. She knew that he had not understood the changes they had made in their family life and was confused and troubled. She prayed silently for help to explain about 'The Song' which had changed their lives.

"It was like this," she began. "As you know, Dad and I have played the fiddle and the guitar since we were small children. One of the things which attracted me to your dad was his love of music. As youngsters we loved to sing and dance around the camp fire, and our families often camped on the same sites. We soon found that we loved to sing and play together and we loved to make up new songs and sing them to the families. After we married, we spent many evenings writing songs and performing them in gypsy ceremonies and celebrations. We were so popular that almost every weekend we were out playing, singing and dancing together. Then, a year or so ago, one night we both woke up with the words in our heads for a new song. They were English, not Romany, words and we hardly understood them. We did not make them up, they were just 'given' to us and so was the tune. It was a beautiful tune, and the words were all about

12

Jesus, who had come to earth to save us all, 'gorgers' and Romanies alike."

"Dad and I were totally amazed," Tyler's mum continued, "Nothing like this had ever happened to us before. We hardly knew who Jesus was, although Romany people are very religious and believe there is a God, we really only knew Jesus as a swear word. The fact that we both had these same beautiful words in our heads and the same exquisite tune running through our minds was so strange; we somehow knew this had been given to us by God. We are not really able to read or write, but it didn't matter, there was no way we would ever forget the words or music. It felt as if angels had sung them to us.

Because we didn't understand what had happened to us, we didn't know what to do or who we should sing 'The Song' to. We knew it must be important somehow, but for a while we just sang it to ourselves before we went to sleep. We were working at a fairground on the south coast at the time. Your Dad, I expect you remember, was helping with the Ferris wheel, and I had a tent and told fortunes."

"Why did you stop doing that?" Tyler interrupted his mother.

"I'll get to that a bit later in the story," she answered. "I had better stop now, anyway, and get on with the cooking and see to little Sunshine. You have some jobs to do for Dad, anyway, and no doubt some homework!"

13

Tyler pulled a face. "Yes, I have to write a story. I wish I could tell a story, it would be so much easier!"

"Romany people are very good at story telling!" his mum commented. "I'll tell you the rest of the 'Song' story tomorrow."

Chapter Three

As soon as school was finished, Theodore grabbed his backpack and jacket and headed to the playground to collect his bike. It was easily the best bike in the shed, he thought to himself, as he put the numbers into the combination lock. Knowing that it was the best didn't make him gloat, but instead it made him feel a little sad because it reminded him of his past life.

Quickly he mounted his bike and began to pedal home. He had to cycle through the village, past the shop, post office, pub and the church and then take the road to the next village, Lesser Syding; which was nothing more than a cluster of houses. There was no shop, pub or church there. The houses once had been the homes for the people who had worked at Syding Castle, where Theodore now lived. He rode through the two stone pillars with their lions on top guarding the entrance to the castle grounds; then up the long drive to the house. The castle was not as big or as imposing as it looked from the road. When Theodore's parents had bought it five years ago it was in a bad state of repair. His father had paid for an army of workmen to get it back into order and to tidy up the park land which surrounded it. A games room for snooker and table tennis had been made out of one of the stables; a heated swimming pool where once there had been a huge greenhouse, and several garages in some outhouses, where his father had kept his collection of classic cars.

As soon as he arrived home Theodore put his bike away in one of the now empty garages and ran in through a side door to the kitchen.

"Hi, Theo," said his mum with a smile. "You must have peddled fast to get home so quickly! Thank you, I can do with your help!"

"Does that mean we have guests tonight?" he asked his mother, who was busy getting him a drink from the fridge.

"Yes," she answered, "We have Mrs Samways here again for three nights and two other couples for one night bed and breakfast. When you have had your drink, can you go and see if the hens have laid any eggs? I need some fresh eggs for their breakfasts."

Theodore's mother looked at her youngest son. She knew how hard things had been for her children since their father left home. The family's lifestyle had changed so much. Her four children had to leave their exclusive private schools and attend the local schools. From being a family who were very well off and had a new 'posh' car every year; holidays abroad in very exotic places; all the latest fashionable gear; ponies to ride and almost everything they asked for, they now had to find a way of managing with very little income. When her husband left home to live with another woman, she had been left with Syding Castle and a million pound mortgage to pay! Her husband sometimes paid a little money for the children's upkeep, but now he lived in Australia and rarely sent to them. The family had been faced with a decision, either to sell the castle and move right away or to make it into a bed and breakfast business in order to have an income. When they decided to do that, the children all knew that they had to work alongside their mother because she could not do all the work on her own. Slowly it was beginning to bring in money, but it was hard work!

"How was your day at school?" asked Theodore's mum.

"Not bad," he answered. He didn't want to upset his mum by telling her the truth. He hated the village school! His classmates made fun of him, calling him 'toffee nose' and 'a swot', as he didn't speak with the same west country accent as they did, and he was miles ahead of them in his school work because when he was at the private school there were only eleven boys in his class.

"I wish we played cricket like we did at St. Augustine's," he said, "Rounders isn't half as much fun!"

"Maybe you should ask your teacher if you can. You never know, he might agree!" replied his mum.

Theodore sipped his drink slowly. He loved these few moments when he had his mum to himself before his brother and two sisters arrived home. Penelope was the eldest and it had been very hard for her to leave the boarding school which she had loved. She had recently celebrated her fifteenth birthday and was very clever, especially at music. She still went to music lessons and hoped one day to get a scholarship to study in London. The twins, Felicity and Sebastian were thirteen and also found it very hard to settle at the local comprehensive school, but they did have each other and did almost everything together.

"Maybe I'll ask him," Theodore said after thinking for a few moments. "Anyway, I'll go and egg hunt. I've got to write a story about an animal, for homework.

"Maybe I can make one up about the chickens or ducks," he added, before he ran outside. Since they decided to use the castle as a bed and breakfast, the family had bought ten chickens and two ducks. They were Theo's responsibility and he had become quite fond of them and liked hunting for the eggs. They did find some funny places to lay them and even though they had a very nice hen house he found very few in there! His main worry was to make sure that the foxes didn't get into the hen house at night.

By the time Theodore had collected the eggs and taken them to the kitchen, his brother and sisters had arrived home from school. He wished they had time to play with him as they used to before Dad left home. Now they had to help in the garden and then do their homework, and there was little time left to play.

"If I help you with the watering tonight, would you have time for a swim?" he asked the twins. They looked at each other and grinned. "Guess we could," Seb answered, "A short one before we do homework."

Theo beamed. "Thanks," he called and ran off to the garden where they were growing vegetables and fruit. It was a warm summer evening and the pool wouldn't be too cold. He just felt like having a splash around!

Chapter Four

*I*t was while he was swimming that Theo had his good, or maybe, not so good, idea. He was fed up with being called a 'swot' and not having any friends at his new school. "I won't bother to do my best any more," he thought to himself. "This story I have to write for homework, I'll just write some silly story. Perhaps if I do badly, the others will like me!"

Theo thought it was a brilliant idea! Why hadn't he thought of it before!! He could have an extra ten minutes swimming now, because his homework would only take a few minutes to do. Theo and the twins raced up and down the pool then had a game with a large ball. They almost forgot the time until they heard their mother calling them for supper. They showered quickly and rushed into the kitchen, looking forward to the spaghetti bolognaise they could smell! After supper they were sent to do their homework while their mother welcomed the guests who were staying the night. Theo used to have a large room on the first floor which had a wonderful view, but when they decided to become a 'bed and breakfast' business, he had to move into a small room. Actually, Theo hadn't minded too much because his new room was in the turret and to reach it he had to climb over a hundred stone stairs which wound upwards in a spiral. A little door lead into his room and he had his own bathroom. It was very private and well away from the guests. He could even play his music loudly and no one could hear!

Theo scribbled a silly story in his English book about a fox stealing a hen. He was surprised that it was quite hard not to do his best and was also surprised that he felt guilty when he finished it quickly and started to play his latest music. He knew that his mum would ask him questions if he appeared too soon to go and shut in the hens for the night! When he thought enough time had passed he ran down the stairs and into the 'snug' as the family called the small sitting room which they used in the evenings. The large lounge was used by the guests, but Penelope was allowed to do her piano practice there if it wasn't in use. Theo could hear her as he ran past. His mother was watching television and smiled as Theo came in.

"Homework all finished?" she asked. "Yes, mum," he answered, "I'll go and put the hens to bed." He went to the back door and across the yard. The chickens knew him well and he soon had them in their henhouse and the padlock on their door. The ducks were next, but they weren't so well behaved! It took Theo quite a few minutes to round them up and shut them in one of the garages for the night. They squawked and fussed so much! Then he went indoors to watch an episode of 'Dad's Army' which he loved. It always made him laugh so much and helped him forget how miserable life was without his dad and at his new school.

Next morning Theo's alarm went off at half past six. He stretched and groaned.

"If only I could have another half hour in bed!" he thought to himself. However, he knew he must get up and be ready for his breakfast. His mother made breakfast for the family first, and then they all helped serve those guests who were up, before they went off to school. Theo knew that Mrs Samways would be up. She came quite often to stay for a few nights. Theo didn't mind serving her, for she was always kind and said 'thank you' and never grumbled that her egg was too hard or too soft; or that her toast was too well done, like some of the other guests. After Theo had eaten his breakfast and cleaned his teeth, he was ready to help. The others had to leave for school earlier than he did. A bus collected them from the castle gates and took them to Dorchester to the comprehensive school.

The bell rang in the dining room and Theo went running in. It was Mrs Samways.

"Hello, love," she said, "It's nice to see you again!" She gave Theo a big smile.

"Nice to see you, too," he answered, "I hope you slept well?" he asked politely in the way his mother had taught him. "What would you like for your breakfast?" he added; then he took her order.

Back in the kitchen his mother cooked the food and he helped carry in things which were not hot. His mum smiled at him gratefully. "I don't know how I would manage without you!" she said, "But now, off you go to school. You mustn't be late!"

Theo said 'goodbye' then grabbed his backpack and jacket before going to the garage to get his bike. He pedalled slowly, not wanting to reach school before the bell went. He didn't want to have to wait around in the playground and have the other kids bully him. Tyler did exactly the same. He dawdled to school, reaching the gate just as the bell went. The two boys who were first to leave were always the last to arrive.

As they entered the door, at the end of the line of children, they bumped into each other by mistake. Theo looked at Tyler as if he hadn't ever really noticed him before.

"Hi, sorry, I didn't mean to bump you," he said. Tyler gave him a shy smile as he replied, "Hi! It's ok, Theodore. No problem!"

"Please call me 'Theo', all my family and friends do," answered Theo. Tyler smiled again; in fact, his whole face beamed. It was the start of a special friendship.

The boys went into the cloakroom together and hung up their coats. Although they had both joined the school in September and now it was May, they had never really spoken to each other before. Suddenly they felt like buddies!

They took their books and pencil cases and walked into the classroom together. The teacher smiled at them both and told the class to settle down ready for the first lesson. Soon it was break time and Theo waited for Tyler before going into the playground. It felt so good to have a friend at last!

"Where do you live?" Theo asked his new friend.

"In Honeysuckle Cottage, on the edge of Gypsy Wood," he answered. "My dad is the manager of the wood, and well, actually, we are Romany Gypsies, but the wood has been called that for years and years," Tyler added.

"Where do you live, Theo?" he asked, wondering if Theo lived near him.

"I live in the next village, Lesser Syding," he answered, not really wanting to say that he lived in a castle in case Tyler thought he was swanking and stopped being friendly. "It's not really very far away and I cycle to school. Do you have a bike?" He asked Tyler.

"Yes, but its rather old and I don't use it very much. It used to belong to my cousin. It's easier to walk through the woods to school and there are so many interesting birds and animals to see on the way. If I rode my bike I would miss them."

"I'd like to come with you into the woods one day and you could tell me about them. Maybe, too, we could go for a bike ride sometime?"

"That would be great!" replied Tyler, as the bell rang to go back to lessons. He suddenly felt very happy. It was the first time that he had a friend to talk with and nobody had pushed or shoved him or called him names!

In the next lesson the teacher asked them to get out the homework he had set them yesterday.

"Before you hand your stories in for me to mark, I wonder if some of you would be brave enough to read them to everyone." Mr Stevens asked, looking around the class for volunteers. A girl called Laura put up her hand. She began to read a very good story about her guinea pig. One day as she was going home from school a fire engine whizzed past her with the siren going. She thought to herself, "I wonder where that is going? I hope it's not to our house!" As she arrived at the house where she lived she saw black smoke coming from the other side of the fence in the back garden, and to her horror she saw that the Scout hall at the back of them was on fire! Her mother was just giving her a hug when there was a loud explosion as a gas cylinder caught fire. It blew away their back fence and Laura realised that the fire could reach their garden shed. Inside the shed was her guinea pig, Gertie. She wanted to run down the garden and try to rescue her, but her mother wouldn't let her. Then there was a knock on the door and a fireman asked if he could get into their back garden with his hoses. Of course Laura's mother agreed, but also told him about the guinea pig. He ran at once and rescued Gertie, bringing her back to the house. Laura cuddled and cuddled the frightened pet, who when all the drama was over was none the worse for her experience.

"That was a fantastic story, well done, Laura!" Mr Stevens commented. Then he looked around the class and his eyes met Theodore's. "How about you, Theodore? He enquired.

Theo was flummoxed! He knew his story was rubbish and he was ashamed of his work, but also this was his chance to prove to the class that he wasn't a 'swot' or 'teacher's pet'.

He stood up and began to read a story about his hens, in very bad English and trying to speak with a Dorset accent like the children in the class. Mr Stevens was puzzled because Theo was one of the brightest pupils, but being a kind teacher he rarely told a child off in front of all the class, so quietly said 'thank you, Theodore' and looked around the class for one more story.

Tyler, feeling so much happier than ever before, stood up and asked Mr Stevens if he could tell his story rather than read it. He proudly told the class that Romany Gypsies were better at telling stories and liked to do so around the camp fire after the evening meal. For once, the children seemed interested and didn't laugh at him as he told them about the red squirrels that used to live in the woods, and what had happened that made them extinct in the local area.

Even the teacher was surprised at how well Tyler told the story. He praised him for doing so.

The rest of the day went quickly for the two boys. They sat together at dinner time and began to find out more about each other. Theo thought all boys supported a football team. His was Chelsea and once he had been to see them play in London! Tyler had never been to a match and told Theo that he didn't know who he would support, as until last year he had travelled all over the country. Perhaps now he should support Dorchester Town, he thought. He told Theo all about his training in boxing, which had started in true Gypsy style when he was only three.

"Do you still train?" asked Theo.

"No," replied Tyler, "I stopped when we came to live in the cottage. In fact, our whole family life changed then. I am not sure if I like it so much now. It's great fun in a caravan travelling from site to site and staying just a few weeks in each place!"

Chapter Five

After school Tyler and Theo were still the first children to leave. Today, though, both felt much happier and raced home to tell their mothers that they had made a friend! Tyler whistled as he ran through the woods. He was quite out of breath when he reached the cottage. Mum was sitting outside as usual, with baby Sunshine on her lap. She looked up at Tyler and was pleased to see he looked happier.

"Tell me about your day," she asked, "You look cheerful!"

"It was great, Mum," he replied. "I have made friends with a boy in my class called Theodore. He said I can call him Theo. He lives in the village of Lesser Syding and cycles to school each day." Mum let Tyler chatter on, pleased to hear about his friend and to see him happy. She put Sunshine into her pram and went to get a drink for her son. He followed her into the house.

"Mum," he asked, "can I bring Theo home one day for tea?"

"Of course you can, dear," she answered, wondering if a gorger boy would want to visit them.

"Good. Thanks, Mum," Tyler answered. "Now, can you tell me the rest of your story about The Song?" he asked.

So they sat together on the front step and his mother continued where she had left off the day before.

"Dad and I realised that we could not just keep this wonderful song to ourselves. It had been given to us for a purpose. We decided to talk to God, even though we had never done that before, and ask him what to do. We now know that we were praying, but then we had no idea! Soon afterwards we were at a big gypsy get together for about a week. One evening we heard a group of Romanies singing, and they were all songs about God. Quickly we went to our vardo and got our instruments, then ran back to join the group. They made us so welcome and we told them about 'The Song' we had been given. They were amazed and excited. Soon everyone learnt it and sang it with us. The leader of the group explained what it was all about, a love song to Jesus, who is the Saviour of the world. Through that week we learnt about Jesus, the Son of God, who came to live on the earth and died instead of us, so that we could be forgiven and become children of God. It was all very new to us, and there was so much we didn't understand. At the end of the week we both agreed that we wanted to give ourselves to Jesus, in fact, to become Christians. Things have been so different for us since then. We are much happier, even though so many of our relatives don't understand why we felt we needed to make changes in our lives and live in a way that pleases Jesus. That is why I gave up fortune telling. God forbids it in his book, the Bible," Mum added.

Tyler remained silent for a while.

"What about gran? Is she a Christian too?" He eventually asked.

"After a few months, gran saw such a difference in our lives. Dad no longer got drunk and hit me. He no longer fought with every person he met who held a different opinion to him. I began to love him more than ever. All this made gran ask questions and then, she too, wanted Jesus as her friend and Saviour. It is hard for us all, though," explained Tyler's mum, "because we cannot read and so cannot read the Bible to learn more. We would like to belong to a church where people are not scared to welcome gypsies, and where they would teach us more. Your Dad wants you to learn to read so that you can read to us. He also prays that one day he will be able to read!"

Tyler was glad to hear more of the story that had changed his family life so much. He had felt so confused about everything. Maybe he could not only learn to read, but also teach his parents, too. That evening Tyler made a decision that he would really, really try to learn to read and write well and work much harder at school! He was very proud of his Romany gypsy heritage, but sad that the gorgers didn't like them.

Theo rode home as quickly as he could. He had just gone through the gateway to the castle when he saw Mrs Samways, their guest, walking up the drive. She looked so lonely that he got off his bike and began to walk with her.

She smiled at Theo and asked him if he'd had a good day at
school.

"Yes, it was the best day since I started there!" he
answered. "At last I have made a friend!" Somehow it was
easy to talk to Mrs Samways, even though she was quite old.
He could tell she liked young people. Not all their guests
were pleased when they discovered children lived in the
castle!

"Why do you come to visit us so often?" Theo asked the
old lady. "Do you live a long way away?"

"I do," answered Mrs Samways. "I live in the borders of
Scotland, in a wee place called Ettrick. I haven't always lived
there, once I lived in Much Syding and was the post mistress
and shopkeeper. I love it here."

"Why did you move away if you loved it so much, Mrs
Samways?" asked Theo.

"You don't have to keep calling me Mrs Samways, I would
like it if you called me 'Sammy', like my friends do. Would
you do that, Theo?" she asked. Then she continued, "I had
a boy called Norman. His father had died when he was
small. I tried my best to bring him up on my own. In those
days it was very hard, there wasn't much help, so I had to
work very long hours in the post office and shop to make
enough money to keep us. He was very strong willed and
naughty. When he was thirteen he ran away from home,

31

and even though the police hunted high and low, they never found him. I have never seen him since that day."

Sammy paused in her story to wipe a tear away from her eye. "After a while, I could not bear to live here and not see him. I gave up hope of him ever coming home. The police warned me he could be dead, but in my heart of hearts I have always felt he was still alive. I moved to Scotland, but I come back here as often as I can, just in case one day he comes back to look for me! Of course, he is a grown man by now, fifty one years old in September."

Theo was lost for words. He felt so sorry for Sammy. Why did he run off and leave his mum?

"I'm so sorry, Sammy," Theo said, quietly. "I do hope one day you will find him."

By now they had reached the castle and Theo locked his bike in the shed. Sammy watched him, and suddenly Theo wanted to hug her and tell her that he would always be her friend. She was surprised and hugged him back. "That's two new friends you have made in one day!" she laughed and disappeared through the front door.

Theo rushed through the back door and gave his mum a huge hug. He would never run away from home! He told his mum about his new friends, though he didn't tell her Sammy's story.

Chapter Six

Tyler and Theo fast became friends, and began to be known as the 'Two T's' at school. The other children stopped bullying them so much, especially as they knew that Tyler could really box! They both seemed to be happier at school, and their teacher, Mr Stevens was very pleased about that, but he was still worried because Theo wasn't bothering to work properly. Tyler, on the other hand, was suddenly taking an interest, especially in reading and writing. It was all very strange. One day, Mr Stevens decided that it was time to have a talk with Theo.

"Theodore, please can you stay behind for a while after school," he said to him at break time one day, "I need to have a little chat with you."

"Yes, sir," answered Theo rather nervously, "but not for long as I have to help my mother."

So that day, when every one else had gone home, Theo waited behind. Mr Stevens looked at him kindly and asked him what was wrong.

"You are a very clever young man and were always top of the class, but recently your work has not been very good. Is something wrong? Don't you understand what you are being taught? I know this school is very different from your last one, but we care very much that all our pupils are happy and do as well as they can," said Mr Stevens.

There was a silence for a few minutes while Theo thought what to say.

"Couldn't we play cricket instead of rounders?" he asked. "It's a much better game!"

"Well ... I could ask the head, we could think about it ... but that doesn't really answer my question, does it?" Then Mr Stevens went on, "I don't want to send you to the headmaster or ask your mother to come and see me without first giving you a chance to talk to me," he added.

Theo went very red and looked at the floor.

"I hated it here because the kids all made fun of me and called me names like 'swot' and 'toffee nose'. I decided if I didn't bother with my work, they would like me better and be friends," he mumbled.

"But," Theo added, "it's a lot better now, because Tyler is my friend. They all called him names, too, like 'dirty gypo'. Romanies are not dirty and are not liars and thieves, like people think!"

"I know they are not, but many people are rude and prejudiced against anyone who is different to them. You have let them win, giving in to them, by not bothering with your school work. I thought you were stronger than that!" replied Mr Stevens. "I am glad you have made friends with

Tyler. He is working so hard and you could help him rather than show him a bad example!"

"Yes, sir," said Theo. He felt ashamed of himself. He knew he had let himself down. He certainly did not want his mother called to the school. She had enough worries as it was. "I'm sorry, sir, I will think about what you have said. Please don't tell my mother."

"Well, Theo," replied the teacher, "let me see that you have changed and we'll forget all about it. I won't forget to think about cricket, though. Maybe that is a good idea! Now off home with you before your mother rings to find out where you are and I have to tell her I kept you in!"

Theo ran out of the door and cycled home as fast as he could!

Maybe he was thinking about the things Mr Stevens had been talking about, or maybe he just wasn't concentrating on the road very well, but, as Theo rode home he was startled by a white van that drove past him at a speed much too fast for a country road, and made him wobble and fall off his bike. All he saw was a dirty back door where someone had drawn a face and written, 'wash me!' Fortunately neither he nor his bike were damaged, but he felt very cross. "I could have been badly hurt," he fumed to himself, as he got back on his bike and rode the rest of the way home. He became even angrier when he arrived home to find the white van outside the castle. He hoped the driver wasn't a guest, because he didn't feel like being polite!

In fact the driver and his mate had checked in for a night. Theo resented going to hunt for eggs for their breakfasts, but he didn't tell his mum why, or she might not let him ride to school any more! Talking to the chickens and ducks calmed him down and by the time the others came home from school he was his usual cheery self and had almost forgotten the incident. After supper Theo went up to his tower room and was about to have his favourite music blaring out, when he remembered his homework. He wanted to do it properly again. He thought it would be easy, but found that it was much harder to get back on track than he had expected. He was still working hard when Seb came up to find him to ask if he wanted a swim.

"I'd love one, but I'm a bit stuck," he answered. "What do you know about ancient hill forts in this area?"

"Not a lot," said his brother, "but I'll help you 'Google' it on the computer if you like after we have had a swim."

"Will you? Oh, thanks so much!" Theo was delighted. His brother didn't usually bother to help him. They went downstairs and bumped into the two men from the white van, who were going out.

"Nice place you have here," they commented. "Are there many farms around. Do you have any which belong to the castle?"

It seemed a bit of a strange question to the boys, but Seb shook his head.

"There are no farms attached to the castle. But of course there are lots of farms in the area. This is the west country!" he answered, and told them the names of nearby farms.

"Are you interested in farming, then?" asked Theo.

The men looked at each other. "Well, sort of," one of them answered. "We are just off for a drive around. See you."

They got in the van and drove off at speed down the drive.

"Funny, but I don't like those guys very much," commented Seb.

"Nor do I," replied Theo. "They drove past me so fast as I was coming home from school that I fell off my bike. I know it was them because of the writing on the back door! I didn't tell mum because she'd only worry!" he added.

Felicity joined the boys and they had a great time in the pool, then as good as his word, Seb helped Theo find out about hill forts on the computer. They were amazed at how many there were in the area!

"Now I think I know what I would like for my birthday. Mum keeps asking me. I would like a metal detector! I could visit the hill forts as well as the sea shore. That would be fun, especially in the school holidays as we can't go away this year!" said Theo, and ran into the kitchen to tell his mum. She seemed slightly amused at such an unusual present, but promised to look into it and see if she could afford it. "No promises!" she said, "But I'll do my best if you are sure that is what you want. Now off to bed with you! I'll need your help with breakfasts in the morning!"

Next day, Theo told Tyler about his idea for his birthday present. He also told him about the white van and the two men who were so interested in farms. He didn't know why, but it all seemed slightly odd. It was almost half term and they were looking forward to a week off. They planned to spend as much time together as possible. Tyler had promised to show Theo how to look for animal tracks in the woods, and Theo had promised Tyler they could play in his turret room. He had also asked Tyler if he could help him with his reading and Theo had so many books in his room, there were plenty that Tyler could borrow.

"Well, actually," Tyler said, "have you got a Bible?"

"A Bible?" queried Theo. "I think I have one somewhere that my Godmother gave me. That's a funny book to want to read. I have far more exciting adventure stories at home!" he added.

"I have a special reason for wanting to be able to read the Bible. I'll tell you sometime," Tyler promised.

The days were sunny and warm for the end of May. Two days before they broke up it was Theo's birthday. He was excited. Somehow being eleven seemed much older than ten! He was up and dressed in plenty of time to help his mother get the breakfasts for the two guests who were staying at the castle.

"No, not today!" said his Mum. "Today is your special day. Open your cards and presents, and I will cook your breakfast first!"

By his plate was a pile of cards and some presents. Theo tore the paper off the largest, whooping with delight as he discovered the metal detector!

"Oh, thanks, Mum, thanks so much!" and he gave his mum a hug.

There were several cards from relatives and family friends. Theo looked at them, hoping against hope that one might have an Australian stamp and be from his father. He tried to hide his disappointment when there was none. His grandparents had sent a cheque for him to buy a present for himself. Then, there was a football game for his games console from his uncle and aunt. He was admiring this when Seb and Flick rushed in singing 'Happy Birthday' at the tops of their voices and gave him a parcel. Inside was a CD of his favourite pop group that he had wanted for ages. He was so pleased and thanked them both. Penny then came into the kitchen and presented him with a new pair of swimming goggles! It was a wonderful day!

His sisters and brother gobbled their breakfasts and rushed off to get the bus to school, which gave Theo a few moments alone with his mum.

"Thank you so much, mum," he said. "You are the best mum in the world!"

She hugged him and then sent him on to school. Birthday or not, it wouldn't do to be late for registration!

Tyler was waiting at the school gate for him. He had a small package. "Happy birthday! I hope you like it," he said nervously as he held it out to Theo. Theo opened it and was amazed. Inside was a carved robin, and it was also a whistle.

"It's beautiful!" exclaimed Theo. "I just love it!"

"I carved it myself," explained Tyler shyly, "Or most of it. Dad helped me with a little bit!"

"You made it! You are so clever! I shall always keep it in my pocket as a treasure!" Theo promised.

The school bell rang and the 'Two T's' went into the classroom together. Tyler's present had made Theo forget for a few moments, his disappointment that his father had forgotten his birthday.

Chapter Seven

Half term week was warm and sunny, and although Theo's mum had quite a few guests, she managed to find time to take her family and Tyler to the beach. It was a chance for Theo to try out his metal detector properly. They had a swim, but the sea was still very cold and they didn't stay in long! Then, after a picnic lunch the two T's went along the beach to see what they might find, while the others sunbathed and fished in the rock pools.

After a little while, the machine began to buzz! The boys started to dig, and unearthed a bottle top! That was a bit disappointing!

"Well, it's not exactly buried treasure, but it's a start!" laughed Tyler. They continued on their walk and found a penknife; a rusty key on a ring; two ten pence pieces and an old nail file. The boys thought it was great fun and decided they would go around the castle grounds and the old hill forts near their village. Who knows what they might find!

On their way home, after a lovely day out, a white van raced round a corner, overtook and almost hit them! Theo's mum was quite shaken.

"How stupid to go so fast on these country roads!" she exclaimed. "We could have had a nasty accident!"

Theo looked at the disappearing van and remarked that it

looked like the one which the two men who'd stayed with them had driven, because he was sure it had a face drawn on the back door.

"I doubt it," said Felicity, "There are so many white vans and they all look the same! Most of them are dirty, too!" she added.

Then Theo told them how he had fallen off his bike because they had driven so fast along the road as he had been coming home from school one day.

"It's funny," said Seb, "but I just didn't like those guys. I felt they were up to no good. Remember all the questions they kept asking about the farms around here. It was sort of weird!"

"Well, they were good guests and paid their bills without any trouble. I think you kids may be letting your imaginations run away with you!" mum commented. So they forgot all about the incident and soon reached home. Penny went to do her music practice, but the other four decided to play cricket as Tyler wanted to learn the game. Afterwards, they had a warm swim in the pool. After supper Theo's mother decided to drive Tyler home, rather than let him ride his old bike through the woods, as it was beginning to get dark. When they arrived at Honeysuckle cottage Tyler's mother was still sitting outside, and she looked very worried.

"I'm sorry if we have kept Tyler out too late," said Theo's mum. "I should have rung you, we didn't mean to worry you."

Tyler's mother looked up. "No, it's fine," she said. "I know Tyler is safe with you and I am so glad he has a good friend." She smiled at Theo. "It's just that we have a problem. The police have been round and taken away my husband for questioning. Some farm vehicles have been stolen, and of course, when gypsies live in the area they are always the first suspects. I know that some Romanies are thieves, just as some gorgers are, but we always seem to be the first to be blamed! My husband Bill, has been at work all day, and is as honest as the day is long, but the police will no doubt give him a rough time!"

"I'm so sorry," said Sally, Theo's mum. "If there is anything we can do to help, please let us know. The boys want to play together tomorrow. It's ok with me and I'll fix them lunch and bring Tyler home before dark. Have you got a mobile number and then we can keep in touch?" she asked. She and Theo had to leave quickly because the others were on their own, apart from Mrs Samways, who was by now, almost like one of the family.

After they had gone, Tyler sat on the step with his mum, who was almost in tears. "Dad will be alright, you'll see!" he said, giving his mum a hug. "I'll take care of you until he gets back," he added, feeling very grown up. "Anyway, you told me we could speak to God about all our problems, so why don't we do that now?" he suggested.

"Oh yes, Tyler, of course we should!" answered his mother. "Let's just do that now, then I must check on baby Sunshine and even though it's holidays, you must get to bed. I am so glad you have such a good friend to play with! I want to hear all about your day!"

Sitting on the step they closed their eyes and Tyler's mum asked Father God to take care of his dad and bring him home safely. Tyler had never said a prayer before, but he added, "And God, please let the real criminals be found and caught, Amen."

They went inside, Tyler chattering about the day at the beach and then learning to play cricket with Theo and the twins. As he was getting ready for bed he heard his father's footsteps coming along the path, then the door open followed by his mum giving a cry of relief. Dad was home and he could go to sleep happily. Maybe, he thought, there really was a God who heard their prayers.

Meanwhile, back at the castle, Theo was telling his sisters and brother and also Mrs Samways, what had happened.

"It was on the local TV news," said Mrs Samways. "A tractor worth thousands was stolen in broad daylight from a farmer's field quite near here. There have been a lot of farm vehicles stolen , 'rustled' I think they called it, in the west country. Now farms in Dorset are being targeted. It must be a gang, from what they said."

44

"Well, one thing is certain," decided Seb, "There is no way that a tractor will fit into a white van, so our guests are probably in the clear!" Mrs Samways was looking a little bewildered when he said this, so Felicity explained about the white van.

"I think it is the same one," she said, "because I have seen it when I have been out walking, and I recognised the men. I guess they just have other business round here."

The next day was drizzly, so when Tyler arrived the boys decided to stay indoors for a while. Everyone was relieved to learn that Tyler's father had been released without charge the evening before.

The two 'T's' equipped with coke and biscuits went up to the turret. Tyler was fascinated by Theo's room. You could see for miles around from the little window, and make as much noise as you liked without being heard! For a while they listened to their favourite boy band, but then Theo remembered that he had promised to help Tyler with his reading. Next term they would be going to the senior school and he didn't want his friend to be laughed at because he struggled to read.

"Did you look for a Bible?" asked Tyler.

"No, I completely forgot!" answered Theo, but let's have a look. I am sure there is one somewhere!" They looked along the shelves, and Theo found a Bible story book which he had been given years ago. "Will this do?" he asked his friend.

"I am sure it will," replied Tyler. "Do you know, I think there is something in this God business." And he proceeded to tell Theo about praying last night with his mum.

The boys didn't quite know where to begin, but when they saw a picture of lions, decided to read that story. It was about Daniel who was thrown into a den of lions because he refused to make his petitions and pleas to the king and continued to pray and give thanks to his God as he had done previously.

"That was a really cool story!" commented Theo. "I had no idea there were good stories in the Bible; I thought it was all boring stuff about rules and regulations we ought to keep!"

"Thank you for helping me," said Tyler, "You really are a great friend and you never call me names like the others!"

"That's because they are ignorant and prejudiced. If they really got to know you, they would want to be friends!"

The weather had cleared and the boys saw the sun coming through the window.

"Lets go for a bike ride!" suggested Theo. "I'd like you to help me now and show me animal tracks and things like that."

Chapter Eight

The boys, armed with a picnic lunch, rode their bikes down to the woods. It was lovely riding through the trees which looked so beautiful in the spring time. They found an old log, sat on it and ate their picnic, then Tyler began to show Theo all the different leaves and how to recognise trees. He was looking out for tracks, too. Because the ground was still damp he soon found some squirrel paw marks and showed them to his friend. He saw some dog prints, too, and was slightly puzzled because he didn't recognise them. He knew almost every dog in the area from their paw prints. Then, he noticed large footprints going away from the path, deep into the woods.

"Let's follow these," Tyler suggested. "They will be easy to follow and good practice for you." The boys followed the footprints deep into the woods, pretending they were private detectives and chasing a criminal. After a while they entered a clearing and saw a sort of make shift shelter made from branches and bracken.

"We'd better be careful," whispered Tyler, "We don't know if someone is still here. It looks like they have a dog. Those paw marks are pretty large!"

The boys quietly went up to the shelter, Tyler considerably more quietly than Theo, who was unused to trekking in the woods. There was no sign of life, but Tyler quickly spotted where there had been a fire. It had been put out, but some of the ashes were still slightly warm.

"There's nothing else here," said Tyler, a little disappointed, as he put his head into the shelter.

"The grass is all flattened though, so my guess is that someone did sleep here last night and has not long gone. I think we had better go back to our bikes. I must tell dad that someone is around."

They walked back, retracing their steps. Theo was glad his friend knew the woods so well. It would be so easy to get lost! All the time he had a strange feeling that he was being watched, but when he looked around he saw no- one. If someone was there, he reasoned, then the dog would have barked at them.

They got back to their bikes and Tyler decided to phone his father, just in case there was someone in the woods who was up to no good. He put his hand into his pocket to get out his mobile but it wasn't there!

"Oh dear!" he exclaimed, "How could I have done that! I must have lost the phone when we went trekking! Do you mind if we go back?"

This time the boys raced back along the track, not worrying at all about being quiet, and soon arrived, a little breathless, at the shelter. There, carefully placed on a tree stump was the phone. It was eerie.

"How did it get there?" Tyler whispered, looking around him, but seeing no one.

"At least it's safe and sound," said Theo, also whispering. "Let's go. I've had enough!"They raced back to the place where they had left their bikes as quickly as they could. Tyler tried to get a signal, but it was very weak and so he gave up.

"I'll just have to tell dad when I get home," he decided.

Once on their bikes they set off to return to the castle. They went through the gateway and Theo smiled at the lions. "They remind me of the story we read, about Daniel," he commented to Tyler.

"That was a good story. Do you think it was really true?" he asked.

"If it's in the Bible, it must be!" answered Tyler. "Mum says that there are stories of all sorts of miracles and says that miracles still happen. I'm not sure if I believe that, though," he added.

They raided the fridge for cold drinks and sat outside sipping them.

"It must be amazing having a home like this, with a swimming pool and everything!" Tyler said, looking around the outbuildings.

"Yes, it is, but I'd do without it all just to have dad back so that we could live as a proper family again. We used to go on holiday abroad and have a new car every year. I don't mind not having those things, but I miss dad. He didn't even send me a birthday card or phone me."

"Anyway, what shall we do now?" he asked Tyler.

"Let's take the metal detector out into the grounds," suggested Tyler.

"Good idea," replied Theo, and went to fetch it. "I'd like to show you my chickens, too. It's about time to collect the eggs."

After collecting the eggs and telling Tyler all about the chickens, Theo collected his metal detector. The grounds around the castle were extensive, so the boys decided to make a plan, so that they could methodically cover the whole area. They began down by the lion gate, working ten strides to the left then ten towards the castle. When the detector began to buzz, the boys realised that they ought to get permission before they dug up the grass. A gardener came each week and he complained a lot about the mole hills and would not be amused if there were a lot of fresh 'diggings' left by boys! So they went up to Theo's room and made their map of the grounds; drew where they had worked and where the detector had buzzed, so that in time, they could investigate the site. Until they had permission to dig, they decided to go metal detecting in places where they could dig without getting into trouble. The woods seemed a good place so they arranged to go back there the next day and see if they could find anything.

After Tyler had gone home, Theo began to look in the bookcases in the lounge to see if he could find a Bible. He couldn't see one, so asked his mother.

"Whatever do you want a Bible for?" she asked. Theo explained that Tyler wanted to learn to read it because his parents were unable to read. He told his mum about reading the story of Daniel. She looked thoughtfully at her son.

"I have a Bible in my bedroom. When I was young I went to Sunday school and I earned it as a prize for good attendance. I used to read it a lot, and there are some very exciting stories in it, but also some things which are very hard to understand. If you really want a Bible, we'll get one when we next go to town," she promised.

That night, before he went to sleep, instead of playing music Theo took the Bible story book off the shelf and began to flick through the pages. He knew the story of Noah's ark, and also Joseph because he had sung in the musical, 'Joseph and his multicoloured dream coat' at his prep school. He began to read about a shepherd boy called David who killed a bear and a lion with his hands when he was looking after the flock of sheep. Was it really true? He must ask Tyler. Then he yawned and fell asleep.

It was hard to get up early in the holidays, but the house was full of guests and Theo knew his mum needed help. He hated to see her always looking so tired! She never went out to restaurants for dinner as she had when dad was at home.

Theo tried to think of when she last dressed up and went to a theatre or a concert. It was months ago! Sometimes he felt so angry with his father and hated him. "One day I will pay you back for being so horrid!" he said out loud, as he dressed.

He helped with the breakfasts, taking in the food and clearing away the dirty dishes. Penelope was helping to cook and the twins were in charge of the dishwasher. Once the guests had gone, Seb and Flick promised to strip the beds and Theo went to start loading the washing machine while Penny and their mum cleaned the rooms and remade the beds. There was so much to do! It was mid morning before Theo was free to meet up with Tyler again. He jumped on his bike and rode to Gypsy Woods, his back pack bulging with his metal detector. It was quiet and cool in the woods, and he dismounted and walked down to Honeysuckle Cottage to meet Tyler. As he went he tried to remember the names of the trees and also look for tracks. He didn't see anything much except that there were still some rather large paw marks and fresh foot prints, so he presumed the dog and his owner were still around.

Tyler was waiting for him. "Sorry to be so long," Theo said, explaining how busy they had been at home.

"That's ok," replied Tyler. "I have been helping dad saw logs and store them for the winter. I was telling him about the shelter we found. He told me that sometimes a tramp stays in the woods for a day or so, but to be careful and always have our phones with us. Did you see anything as you came through?"

"Not really," answered Theo, "I think there are some fresh footprints and paw marks, but I can't be sure."

Tyler's mum, Betty, called them in for a drink, and said she would have lunch ready in an hour.

Tyler knew the woods well. There were lots of small paths which led off the main path . He took Theo down a twisty path. Underneath the beech trees there were still some bluebells and many wild garlic plants which had a strong smell. They came to a clearing and began to use the metal detector, but it didn't react at all so they gave up and instead watched a colony of wood ants busy on a dead tree stump. Theo didn't know that they could sting him with a substance called formic acid. It seemed there was a lot to learn in the woods! Suddenly Tyler stiffened, his whole body alert.

"Shh! Listen," he said softly to Theo. They heard footsteps and the padding of a dog's paws and looked up to see a man with a large German Shepherd dog. For a moment no one spoke. Then the dog began to move towards the boys, growling.

"Come back, Laddie," called the man. He was dressed in a dirty raincoat, tied around the middle with a bit of string. The boys realised he must be the tramp. They felt a little scared. Tyler was the first to speak.

"Hello," he said. "We are watching the wood ants. Was it your shelter we saw yesterday?"

"It was. I saw you there and found your phone. Don't be afraid, Laddie won't hurt you."

"Thank you for putting it on the tree stump," replied Tyler.

"We must go for lunch now," Theo said nervously, remembering he should never speak to strangers. "Come on, Tyler," he said to his friend and began to run down the path.

"Not that way!" said the man, "That is the wrong drum."

Tyler looked at the man sharply. "You speak Romany?" he questioned. "Are you a gypsy?"

"Yes, I speak it, but no, I am not a gypsy. I used the word without thinking."

"Well, we must go, mum has lunch ready. The man's right, Theo, that is not the right path, we need to go this way," Tyler said, pointing in the opposite direction.

The boys ran all the way back to Honeysuckle cottage. Theo was scared. "We shouldn't speak to strangers," he said to Tyler. "Anything could have happened to us down there."

"I know you're right, but he speaks Romany, and he didn't set his dog on us. We'll tell mum when we get in," replied Tyler. By now the boys could see the cottage and slowed down to a walking pace. As they drew near they could hear a commotion.

"Wow, it's gran's vardo!" shouted Tyler in excitement, the tramp suddenly forgotten.

"Look, Theo, see how beautiful it is! There's Sparks, her pony! I wonder why she has come back before the winter!"

The boys ran round to the back of the cottage. Tyler's parents were settling the vardo. Nearby was a large truck and horsebox, and several other people.

"What's happening?" Tyler asked, "Where's gran?"

He realised that his two uncles and some of his cousins were there, but he couldn't see his grandmother. Everyone seemed to be talking at once, and mostly in Romany, so Theo felt very shy and wondered if he should just get his bike and go home. Then Betty, Tyler's mother, came over to the boys.

"We have just had a surprise," she announced. "Gran has not been feeling well, so she decided to come here for a while. Your uncles Joe and Walt brought her vardo in their large truck to get her here quickly."

"Where is gran? Can I see her?" asked Tyler.

"She's resting in the cottage and waiting for the doctor to call, but if you are quiet you can see her. You too, Theo, she will be pleased to meet you," she added. "Once the vardo is settled we will all have lunch."

Tyler's gran was very tiny, with silvery hair and a lovely smile. Theo liked her at once. She gave her grandson a big hug and asked to be introduced to his friend.

"I am so glad you have a friend. Your ma told me you were much happier at school and I am pleased. God has been hearing my prayers!"

"Are you alright?" asked Tyler in a quiet, worried sort of voice.

"I will be, I am sure the doctor will help me. I am glad to be home with you again. I feel safe here.

Now leave me to sleep my dears, and I will see you later."

"Yes, gran," the boys whispered and crept out of the room.

Lunch was a very noisy affair with all the family around. They ate outside around a camp fire, and Theo thought it was marvellous. However, when they heard the doctor's car coming down the lane, Theo felt he should go home. He didn't want to be in the way, so he said goodbye to Tyler and thanked his mum for having him. "I do hope gran will soon be better," he said as he put his metal detector into his back pack and got on his bike.

Chapter Nine

The next couple of days seemed to drag by for Theo, Tyler was busy with his family and couldn't come out to play. It had been so good to have a friend to play with! Half term was almost over and they hadn't done half of what they had planned! Theo amused himself by using the metal detector on the next part of the map which he and Tyler had made, but it wasn't so much fun on his own. Seb and Flick were working on a school project and didn't want to play cricket or swim so he was left to his own devices. It was late on Friday afternoon that he was sure he saw the white van again! Up in his turret bedroom, Theo could see for miles, and he liked to look out using his binoculars. He was sure he saw a white van turn into Cowleaze farm, followed by a truck. He couldn't really be sure it was the same van, but instinct made him feel it was. He stood watching, then, four men went into the long barn. He couldn't see what was happening because the truck obscured his vision. After a while, two men got into the van, and even at a distance they looked familiar, then they drove off at speed down the lane towards Dorchester. A few minutes later the truck also drove off in the same direction. Theo stayed looking, puzzled and somehow sure that what he had seen was important. If only Tyler was around to discuss it!

Thinking of Tyler made Theo wonder how 'gran' was. Somehow, he just thought of her as 'gran'. She was very different from both his 'grandma' and 'nanny', so it seemed alright to call her 'gran'. He got his mobile and sent a text to his friend, then decided he was hungry and almost supper time, so ran downstairs. His mum was busy cooking and it smelt good.

"I was thinking we could go to Dorchester tomorrow and look for the Bible you wanted," she suggested. "Would you like to do that? I need to get some shopping. Maybe we could even go to the cinema."

"That sounds great, thanks, mum. Can you spare the time?" Theo answered. His mum smiled at him. "I will make sure I can," she said. "Penny is having an extra music lesson and the twins are wanting to go to Dorchester to the Museum to work on their project. We only have one visitor booked in this weekend, and we will be back in time to look after her."

Theo was pleased to have something to do the next day. Although the town of Dorchester was only a few miles away, it always seemed like a treat to go there, especially to the cinema! He was pleased, too, to be able to have his own Bible. It must be a special book, he thought, if Tyler's parents had sent him to school to learn to read it!

It took Theo and his mother a little while to choose a Bible, because there were so many different versions. This really mystified Theo, but his mother explained that over the years many people had revised the original translations or made new ones, putting the text into more modern English so that people could read and understand it better.

"I found the one I had as a Sunday School prize but it was hard to understand. I want to get one for myself that I can read easily, as well as getting yours," she said. In the end, she chose a version for herself she could understand and one in slightly easier English for Theo. The matinee film was exciting, too. It was a new version of 'Robin Hood', one of Theo's favourite stories. They munched through popcorn and thoroughly enjoyed themselves! It was on the way back to the car park that Theo noticed a board outside the local newsagent that announced, "Tractor stolen from Cowleaze farm". He remembered seeing the van and truck there and was about to tell his mother when they saw the twins running to them, full of what they had seen at the museum.

Seb and Felicity found it very odd that their mother and Theo should have bought Bibles, but did not tease him when Theo showed them his.

The weekend passed quickly and soon it was Monday and everyone was back to school after the holiday. Tyler came in looking very dejected and Theo thought his gran must be worse. He shook his head when his friend asked how she was.

"She is still poorly but will soon get better," he answered, "We have had a terrible weekend. The police came again and arrested dad and my uncles because another tractor has been stolen. Someone saw a large truck driving along the lanes and decided it must be ours! Nothing would convince the police that we had nothing to do with the tractor theft. Dad and my uncles are held in custody, gran is trying to rest and my cousins are driving mum mad and making Sunshine cry! I was really glad to get back to school!"

"That's terrible!" sympathised Theo. Then he remembered seeing the white van and the truck from his window and told Tyler about it. "I am sure I saw the thieves, it must have been them. But how can we prove it?" he asked.

School seemed to drag that day for the two 'T's'. At the end of the afternoon Mr Stevens called Theo over.

"I have thought about your idea of playing cricket and talked to the headmaster. For a long time now we have wanted to start some 'after school clubs'. If we had a cricket one, would you come?

"I would like to if mum agrees," replied Theo. "I think Tyler would be keen too, because in the holidays my brother, sister and I were teaching him to play."

"Good, I'll get it organised. I thought we might have a textile club as I know some of the girls like to sew and knit, and maybe a Bible club for everyone."

"Mum bought me a Bible in the holidays, because Tyler wants to read it to his parents," said Theo shyly. "They can't read but want to know about the Bible. Perhaps we might be able to come to that club, too."

"That would be really great, Theo," answered his teacher. "I am so glad you two boys have become friends."

Tyler was still in the playground. He looked so unhappy. Some of the girls were skipping together and shouting a rhyme:

> My mother says that I never should
> Play with the gypsies in the wood.
> If I did, she would say
> Naughty, naughty girl to run away!

As they sang they made faces at Tyler. He knew he couldn't fight the girls, but he was very angry with them.

"It's because people are so hateful to my people that my dad and uncles have been put in jail!" he said to Theo. "What can we do to help them?"

"I don't know. I haven't any evidence of what I saw and I bet the police wouldn't listen to me. Everyone knows you are my friend and would think I made it up to help you! I have to go home now to help mum, but if your mum lets you, can you come to mine in about an hour? Maybe if we put our heads together we can think of something. Text me if you can come. Mum will give you supper and we can do a bit of reading from my new Bible."

The boys split up and went home. Theo did his jobs as quickly as he could and was ready when Tyler arrived. They went up into the tower and Theo got out his binoculars and showed Tyler how well he could see the countryside around. He pointed out Cowleaze farm where he had seen the white van and the truck parked. They wished they knew what to do!

"I guess we had better do a bit of reading. I told mum we would be reading the new Bible. Look, it's really cool!" Proudly Theo took down his Bible from his bookshelf and flicked through it. It fell open at the first book of the New Testament. "I had no idea there were so many books in it, or that it was divided into two sections. Mum says it's like a library and the second part is easier to understand than the first. Let's see what this page says," said Theo, looking at where the book had opened. "Matthew ... it's not quite the beginning ... but look! It has a heading: 'Ask, Seek, Knock'."

Theo helped Tyler to read from chapter 7 and verses 7–12.

They puzzled for a while what the verses might mean. "I think 'ask' is about asking God for things, like praying," said Tyler, "and it says here that God will answer."

"Could we ask him about your dad and uncles and how we could help?" suggested Theo.

"'Spose we could. We could give it a try, anyway," answered Tyler.

The boys were quiet and closed their eyes just as they did in school assembly when they prayed.

"God, we ask you to help us find a way to help my dad and uncles and the real thieves to be caught," muttered Tyler.

Then Theo added, "It says in the Bible you will hear us. Thank you. Amen."

They were rather shy at having experimented in this way together, but did decide that they would go to the Bible club when it started so that they could learn more.

After supper Theo had a good idea. "Why didn't I think of it before?" he said to Tyler. "Those men who stayed here who had the dirty white van asked us about the local farms. Let me make a list of the ones we told them about." He got a notebook and wrote down West Down, Cowleaze, High Copse, Salterton's and Castle View.

"I think those were all we told them about. They asked lots of questions about the kind of crops grown or stock kept. They didn't seem very interested in the piggery or the stables."

"Can we see all those farms from your room?" asked Tyler.

"Not Salterton's, but I think you can the others," answered Theo as he got the binoculars again and looked around. "See, Tyler," he said as he handed them to his friend, "on the left is Castle View, then the buildings in the very far distance are High Copse. I showed you Cowleaze and West Down is just past those trees."

"West Down and Cowleaze have both had their tractors stolen," said Tyler thoughtfully. "We must keep an eye on the others. I think God has given us the idea of making a list of the farms. I think he did hear us pray!"

Just then Theo's mum called the boys down as it was getting dark. She put Tyler's bike in the back of her car and

drove him home. Tyler had told her what was happening
at home and she wanted to see Betty and ask if there was
anything she could do to help. The men had been released
as they could not be held without charge any longer, but they
all still felt as if they were under suspicion. Tyler's uncles
and cousins were just about to set off home in their truck.
The two mothers, Betty and Sally, were becoming good
friends through their sons' friendship, even though their lives
were so different.

Chapter Ten

A few days after this, the school clubs were launched. Much to Mr Steven's surprise, most of the boys and a few girls signed up to join the cricket club. He was glad to see Theo so happy and playing with the other boys, and Tyler seemed to be accepted, too. He was proving to be a good bowler! Silently, he thanked his Father, God. He had been so concerned for these two boys and now his prayers were being answered and they seemed happier and were both improving in their school work.

The Bible club was not quite such a hit, but a few children stayed behind, including Tyler and Theo, the vicar's son and daughter, the three children from Castle View Farm and a little girl from the infants' class called Lara. They were a bit shy at first, but soon had a great time playing some games with Mr Stevens and another teacher called Miss Roberts. Then they had refreshments, followed by a Bible story told by Miss Roberts and her puppets. It was so good, that the two 'T's' couldn't wait for the next week to go again!

Almost every day the boys met after school, usually at Theo's home as he had to look after the chickens and help his mum. The evenings were light now and they had lots of fun in the castle grounds. Their map of where they had used the metal detector was getting filled in and there were several places they hoped one day they could dig up. They continued to read the Bible together and kept a close eye on the farms around, but everything appeared to be quiet. Maybe there would be no more tractor thefts.

It was unusual for the middle of summer, but Theo's mother suddenly had a few days without any guests so Theo was able to go to spend time in the woods and at Honeysuckle cottage. The boys were out tracking one afternoon after school when they bumped into the tramp. He was startled when he saw the boys and seemed very upset because he had lost his dog.

"He went missing last night, and I have searched the woods calling for him all day."

The tramp looked so miserable that both boys felt sorry for him.

"Would you like us to help find him, Mister ..." Tyler was just about to say 'Tramp' when he stopped himself. He hated it when people called him 'gypsy', maybe this man didn't like being called a tramp, either.

"Would you?" he asked the boys, "And you can call me Sam. My dog is Laddie."

"Yes, we remember that," said Theo. "If we find him, where shall we bring him?"

"To the clearing where I left your phone that day. I shall sleep there tonight."

The boys left Sam and started down a small path that led to the middle of the woods.

They called as they went and also looked for any sign of paw marks, but the ground was dry and they could see nothing. They were about to give up and go home when they heard a whine. It was very faint and seemed to come from deep within the earth! They called again and listened to the answering whine, then moved to where they thought the noise was coming from. They did this several times and then Tyler discovered a half hidden deep hole. He peered in and saw the dog inside. The boys could see that Laddie was both hurt and frightened. They tried to reach down to help him out, but he growled at them. The brambles were scratching them and the hole was so deep they didn't want to fall into it. Tyler decided they needed to get help. Theo used his mobile to ask his mum to get the vet who used to look after their horses, while Tyler ran back first, to tell Sam the good news and then, to the main path in the woods to meet the vet when he arrived.

Theo stayed near the hole and talked softly to the injured dog. It seemed to calm him and the dog stopped whining all the time. After a while he heard rustling in the trees and Sam appeared.

Sam was so pleased that Laddie was found and happy to hear his bark when he called to him.

Theo was sitting on an old tree trunk and the tramp joined him.

"Thanks for finding him. Laddie is all I have in the world!" he told Theo. They were silent for a while, and then Theo's curiosity got the better of him.

"Tell me about being a ..." he hesitated a little, then said, "Tramp. Why do you come here to our woods and village?"

"Oh, son," Sam replied, "it's a long and not a very happy story. But I will tell you, so that you will never be as stupid as I was at your age! I guess it will help the time to pass while we wait for the vet."

"When I was just a youngster my dad died and inside I was very angry and became a real naughty boy. My poor mum couldn't manage me and I wouldn't help her or do what I was told. Eventually, I ran away from home, thinking I would go to London and one day become rich! Only, I met up with gypsies camping in these woods and at first they were very nice to me and told me I would be like their son and travel the country with them. Before they left here they robbed the village post office. I was terrified because my mum was the post mistress! When they found that out they kept me like a prisoner, so that I couldn't grass on them. I was only thirteen, and my life quickly became like hell. We travelled all the country alright, but I was made to do all the dirty and heavy chores, and even help with some burglaries. This went on for years. I learnt to speak Romany and most people thought I really was one of them. We were at a fairground in Scarborough one time and I managed to escape. I had planned it for ages, and that is when I became a 'man of the road'. I headed to Scotland because I knew the family who had captured me didn't travel up there. I managed to get odd jobs from time to time, and wandered around. After several years, I started to travel back down to the south, always avoiding places where gypsies camped, except for here where I came every year. I just wanted to know if my mother was still alive, maybe just to look at her from a distance. I knew she would never recognise me as the boy she once knew. I could never go home because everyone must have thought I had robbed my own mother, and I couldn't bear that! I had nothing to do with it. Anyway, she hasn't lived here for years as far as I know and I am sure she is probably dead, but this is the only place I have known as 'home' and the only happiness I had in my life. In my anger I threw it all away! If only I could turn the clock back!" Sam looked away from Theo, trying not to let the boy see the tears in his eyes!

Theo was bubbling over with excitement! "But she is alive! Your mum I mean! She comes to stay at our house every few weeks." The words were tumbling out and Theo was not sure that he was making any sense. "We run a bed and breakfast, and this lady called Sammy, I mean, Mrs Samways, who is quite old, comes and walks around just in case her boy who ran away when he was thirteen, comes home! Only his name is Norman and he will be 51 in September."

The tramp looked at Theo as if he couldn't believe his ears! "My name is Norman, but everyone called me 'Sam' as my surname was Samways. You mean my mum is alive!

She still looks for me?" The tramp screwed his face up, and then he began to sob like a baby. Theo was embarrassed and reached into his pocket to get a crumpled tissue.

"I'm sorry, son," he said as he blew his nose and wiped his dirt streaked face. "I never thought she was alive and I would see her again."

They suddenly heard voices and Tyler came along with the vet and the difficult operation of rescuing Laddie from the hole, began. It appeared the dog had broken his leg and was in a lot of pain. The vet said he would have to take him to the surgery for treatment. Sam looked at first relieved and then dismayed.

"I have no money for operations and such," he began to explain.

"Don't worry about that. The first thing to do is to help your dog. I do have a fund for people who really can't pay," replied the vet.

At this moment Bill, Tyler's dad, appeared.

"How are we getting on?" he questioned the vet, and was soon put in the picture. He went over to the deep hole and peered inside.

"I shall have to fill this in at once. Someone could get hurt if they fell in there." He pulled out a torch and shone it into the hole. "Goodness!" he exclaimed, "there seems to be a large bag down there. I think the dog may have been trying to eat it or something because it is partly falling to pieces. I shall have to investigate." And he started to climb down into the hole.

"Heavens above!" he exclaimed, "The bag contains tools, bank notes, postal orders and even old stamps! I think we had better call the police!"

Sam began to shake and Theo was sure he was going to break down again. He thought he should get Sam to tell his story to everyone.

"Sam has told me about himself and I think he ought to share his story with everyone while we wait for the police," decided Theo.

"Well, I need to get Laddie to the surgery. You can wait without me. How can I contact you Sam when it is all over?" asked the vet.

Tyler and his dad looked at each other. "You can stay in our caravan for the time being," said Bill. "The vet can phone us and we can take you to the surgery."

While they waited for the police to arrive, Sam retold his story for Tyler and his dad. They were amazed! "So you think this haul may be from that post office robbery all those years ago!" said Tyler, "And fancy you being Mrs Samways's lost son!"

It was getting late, Theo had text his mum to say he would be late for supper, but had a reply to say she was coming to pick him up. That wasn't what he wanted at all! He didn't want to miss the excitement! In the end, the police arrived before his mum, and having heard all the story, put a cordon around the hole and told everyone to go home. They told Sam to stay at Honeysuckle cottage just in case they needed to question him further, and for once, they were polite to Tyler and his dad! Theo had so much to tell his mum on the way home! Back at the castle his mum looked up Mrs Samways's telephone number in Scotland and allowed Theo to talk to her.

"Sammy," he said, "it's Theo at Syding Castle here. I have found your son, Norman. He is so wanting to see you, but also afraid. I told him you would love to see him because you always come looking for him. Can you come back really soon and meet him?"

Mrs Samways was quite overcome, and Theo's mum took over the phone and tried to explain a little more.

"I will get the train tomorrow and reach you by the evening. That is, if you have room for me," she added.

"Of course we do! We are not at all busy just now. Why don't you ring us from the station and we will come to Dorchester and collect you," suggested Theo's mum. It was agreed that was what they would do.

Chapter Eleven

*B*oth Tyler and Theo were bubbling over with
excitement at school the next day! Tyler told Theo
that Laddie had his leg in plaster and was going to stay
along with his master in their caravan. He giggled as he told
Theo that Sam had spent an hour in the bath and came out
wearing some of his dad's clothes! He had cheered gran up
so much when he told her his story, talking mostly in the
Romany language. She thought it was wonderful. "Good
enough for a book!" she had said.

Theo told his friend how he had talked to Sammy on the
phone and that she was travelling down today. "Better not
tell Sam yet," cautioned Theo, "in case he decides to back
out and runs away again. Mum says she will talk to your
mum and arrange somewhere private for them to meet."

Mr Stevens noticed the two 'T's' were very excited and
finding it hard to concentrate in class. They were due to
be staying for Bible club that evening, but at the end of
school when he reminded the children about club, both boys
wanted to get home quickly. They tried to explain to their
teacher about their amazing discovery of Mrs Samways' lost
boy, but the story was so complicated that he couldn't make
head nor tail of it all! A dog with a broken leg, a lost tramp,
a post office robbery! He thought their imaginations were

working overtime, but sent them home with a smile and said he hoped they would come next week!

When Tyler got home he found that Laddie and Sam were the centre of attention. The police had called round to say that they had retrieved the post office haul and the tools, and had sent them for forensic examination. They had talked to Sam at length and believed his story, much to his relief. Laddie was asleep at his feet and looked so funny with a plaster cast on his leg and a large white collar around his neck to stop him licking it! They warned Sam that the local press would probably be around once they heard the story!

Theo rode home as quickly as he could, hoping that he would be in time to go to the station with his mum. He breathed a sigh of relief to see her 'four by four' still in the drive.

Running into the kitchen he saw his mum was getting ready to go.

"Wonderful!" she exclaimed. "Sammy has just phoned, so we can go to Dorchester. I told the others to meet us at the station after school. What a wonderful day for her!"

It was indeed a wonderful day for Mrs Samways. She got off the train as if she were young again, and hugged all the 'castle' family warmly, especially Theo.

"Now you must tell me all about how you found my Norman. I want to know every little detail!" she said.

Theo told her all he knew, from the day they went tracking in the woods until he had left Sam at Tyler's home last night, even about the bath and the borrowed clothes! Everyone was so pleased and excited for Sammy.

"We do have a problem now," Theo explained, "I shall get so muddled calling you Sammy and Norman, Sam!"

"That's the least of our worries, we will work something out," laughed his mum.

As soon as they arrived home, Sammy wanted to know when she could meet her son.

Sally made a call straight away to Betty, Tyler's mum. She had an update on all that had taken place during the day, and both mums decided the pair must have a quiet place to meet and be on their own. They put their heads together and decided that gran's vardo was so cosy and pretty, yet enough away from the cottage, and would be perfect for a reunion. That evening, after thirty eight long years, a mother and son were reunited! A few days later the police confirmed that none of Sam's fingerprints were on the haul from the bank robbery and they were delighted that one of their old investigations was reopened and they had new evidence.

For a little while the village was buzzing with the news of Mrs Samways and her son. Some of the older folk remembered her and the post office robbery. The press even interviewed the two 'T's', and all the children in the school suddenly wanted to be their friends! Eventually, the fuss died down and the boys were glad to be back to normal. Mrs Samways took Norman and Laddie to be with her in Scotland, but promised to return before too long, for a visit.

The after school club for cricket was a surprising success and soon there was a school team, with Theo as the captain. He was very proud to be the opening batsman and practiced hard after school, most days. Tyler was usually with him, practising his bowling. They had become inseparable friends! They still read together and were amazed at how interesting the Bible was!

One day, at the Bible club, the group looked at chapter fifteen of St.Luke's gospel, the third book of the New Testament. They read about the one lost sheep from a flock of a hundred. The children from Castle View Farm were very interested in this story. They told everyone how their dad cared even for the weakest lambs and how they helped to bottle feed them in lambing season. It made perfect sense to them that a shepherd would leave the ninety nine sheep in a fold and go out to look for a lost one.

Then they read and talked about the woman who had ten coins and lost one. The teacher explained how precious these coins would have been, and how they were a dowry and worn across the forehead, much as today a woman might wear a very precious necklace. They stopped and acted out this story, pretending to sweep and search for the coin. When they had found it, Mr Stevens and Miss Roberts produced some lovely cakes to enact a party to celebrate the coin being found. Finally, they read the story of the son who ran away, and his big brother who was so jealous. The two 'T's' were amazed. It was just like the story of the tramp, who they still thought of as 'Sam', but were trying to call 'Norman'. The group discussed what may have made the son run away from home. They decided he wanted to have a good time and buy everything he wanted, like the latest gear that was available in those days. For a few minutes Theo was silent. Then he told everyone Norman had run away from his mum because he felt so angry inside and rebellious towards everyone and everything. He admitted that there were times when he felt really angry with his father and hated him for what he had done to his family. "I didn't want to run away from home, but I get so angry I want to kill him!" he confessed. "I feel really sorry about it."

Mr Stevens seemed to understand and told the group that Jesus had told the three stories to help people understand how much he loved them and wanted them to be in his family. He was always looking for them, and like the son who ran away, we can come to him and say we are sorry, and he will forgive us and we can live as his children in his family, even though we don't deserve it.

"However," he reminded them, "don't forget the elder brother. He chose to remain jealous and stay away from the party. We have the choice to say sorry and give our lives to Jesus, or to walk away from him and do our own thing!"

All the way home, Theo was feeling bad about the hate and anger in his heart. He knew it was eating away at him. He looked after his chickens and ducks, had supper and did his homework, but all the time thoughts were spinning around in his head. "If I say sorry to Jesus for my hate and anger then it means I have to forgive my dad, and that's not fair! Look how he has treated us! Look at poor mum working so hard and always so tired! Surely God doesn't expect me to forgive him!" Yet deep inside Theo knew if he were to say sorry for his hate and really mean it, then he had to forgive his father. All evening he kept thinking about the lost son and also what being angry had done to Mrs Samways's son so long ago. He didn't want to end up like that! At bedtime he read the stories once again in his own Bible. How glad Theo was that he was away from everyone and in his turret room, for he began to sob and, let all the hate and anger out. Eventually, he felt he could say sorry to Jesus and ask him to forgive him and come to be his friend and Saviour. Although he knew his dad was far away in Australia, he said out loud, "I don't understand why you left us, but I forgive you, dad." After this Theo felt almost happy, and went off to sleep as soon as his head touched the pillow, not counting sheep, but dreaming of the shepherd who went looking for the one who was lost.

Chapter Twelve

As the summer term progressed, the two 'T's' found they were making many more friends at school. The three children, Paul, Tim and Tessa, who lived at Castle View Farm and went to the Bible club, were especially friendly and invited Tyler and Theo to visit the farm and have tea one Saturday afternoon. They rode to the farm on their bikes and had a fabulous time exploring and then playing 'hide and seek' in the outbuildings. The children's mother, Mrs Jenkins called them in for tea. They washed their hands under the pump in the yard, before going into the large kitchen. What a spread there was! They sat down and Mr Jenkins appeared from the dairy, having just finished the afternoon milking. He was very pleased to meet the two 'T's'and before they went home promised to show them a calf which had been born that day. It was black and white, a Friesian heifer, and sucking from its mother. It had been such a lovely afternoon and both boys were sad when it came to an end and they had to cycle home.

They had ridden about a quarter of a mile when they saw a white van coming in the opposite direction, being driven very fast. Suddenly alert, Theo managed to see the registration: WIK 58 FOR. He was sure it was the van which belonged to the men who had stayed at the castle for B&B.

"Stop," he said to Tyler, who was freewheeling down the hill. "Stop, Tyler. I think we should go back to the farm. I am sure that is the same white van. What if it is going to Castle View Farm to steal a tractor? We must warn the Jenkinses!"

Tyler stopped and the boys turned around and began to pedal back up the hill. Theo had to slow down because Tyler didn't have a mountain bike with loads of gears like his, and it took him much longer. They went around the next corner and saw the van had pulled into an entrance to a field. There were two men and one of them was on the phone.

Quietly, the boys dismounted, hid their bikes in the hedge, then climbed through a gap and managed to get into the field without being seen. Tyler's lessons in tracking had proved useful, for both boys could move almost as quietly as red Indians! They crept up under the hedge until they could hear what the man was saying on his mobile.

"We are just by the farm," he said, "Drive the truck and park in the lay-by until the light begins to fade. There is a dog, but I will take care of him with poisoned meat. The vehicle we want is not in the farm yard but just passed it in the first field. You will have to drive into the entrance and we will be there to help."

The boys looked at one another, their eyes wide with horror.

"They are going to poison Rover! We have to stop them!" whispered Tyler.

"Yes, but how?" answered Theo.

"We have to creep past the gate and make our way to the farmhouse to warn the Jenkinses." Having said this, Tyler quietly began moving past the gate, but as he did so, one of the men turned towards it to open it. He knocked Tyler over and immediately Theo went to help his friend. A hand grabbed him and another was clasped over his mouth just as he was about to scream 'help!' The other man got hold of Tyler, whose head was bleeding caused by the gate hitting him.

"Well, look who it is!" said the man holding Theo, "That snooty little kid from the castle! What were you doing snooping around the hedge?" he asked roughly.

Without thinking, Theo blurted out, "We were going to stop you from poisoning Rover!"

"You were, were you? So you heard our plans! We had better take care of you two then!"

The boys were taken to the van, with their hands tied together and rags tied around their mouths to keep them quiet. They were locked in the back of the van. They heard the men talking together for a while, and then it became quiet. The boys feared that they had gone to dope Rover. Theo felt so bad that he had blurted out Rover's name, and also that he had let Tyler down. If only he had kept his mouth shut! He felt like crying, but knew that wouldn't help anyone, so he began to wriggle his nose and mouth in an attempt to loosen the gag and speak to his friend. Tyler began to copy him, and in spite of being afraid, they wanted to laugh as they both looked so funny! It didn't work, they still couldn't talk! Then Theo had another idea. His feet had also been tied together, but he managed somehow to get on his knees, then he looked at Tyler and closed his eyes. Tyler got the message. They could pray! Both boys silently called out to God to help them and rescue them, Rover and Mr Jenkins's tractor!

Back at Syding Castle Theo's mum was getting worried. Theo was always very good about coming home in good time and if plans changed, he phoned her or sent a text. She called Betty and Bill, only to find they were also worried as it was beginning to get dark. Gran promised to look after Sunshine while Tyler's parents drove to the castle. Both mums were agitated and crying. Bill suggested that they phone the boys on their mobiles. "Why hadn't I thought of that?" Theo's mum said.

The phones were ringing, but there was no answer. Then they phoned the Jenkins and learnt the boys had left there about two hours earlier.

"Why don't you come over here right away? I will have a look around the farm buildings. I showed them a new born calf earlier, perhaps they have gone back to see it," Mr Jenkins said reassuringly.

Bill, Tyler's dad, took control.

"Betty," he decided, "You stay here with the twins and Penny. You can answer the phone if they ring home and let us know. We will keep in touch."

So Theo's mum went with Bill and they drove up to the farm. They were relieved not to see any evidence of an accident but as it was now dark they didn't see the bikes hidden in the hedge or notice the white van still parked in the gateway to the field. Mr Jenkins met them as they drove into the farmyard. He had searched the outbuildings without any success.

"Strange thing is," he remarked, "our dog Rover seems to have gone missing, too. If Rover is with them, he is a good guard dog and will look after them. I think it is time to call the police. Before we do, I would like to do one other thing, if you will let me. I am a Christian and believe in prayer. God, my Father, knows where the boys are. Let us ask for his help and also his protection over them."

"I would like that," said Bill, at once, and Theo's mum nodded through her tears. Anything to bring her son back safely!

After a simple prayer, to which they all said 'amen', Mr Jenkins phoned the police.

He gave them clear directions to the farm, but they warned him it would take maybe twenty minutes or so for them to come out from Dorchester.

Chapter Thirteen

*I*t was now dark in the van and both boys were cold
and tired. They were almost dropping off to sleep
when the door opened.

"Companion for you!" said one of the men, and threw in
Rover, who seemed either asleep or dead. The boys couldn't
touch him, so they had no idea.

With the door still open both men lit a cigarette. "We must
decide what to do with these kids," one of them said.

"They know too much," the other one answered. "Maybe
we will have to ask the others. They won't be happy about
this complication! Anyway, lets go and finish the job," he
continued as he heard his phone beep with a message. "That
means they are up at the field."

They locked the van again and the boys heard the footsteps
of the men disappear up the lane.

The parents and the Jenkinses found it hard to sit and wait
for the police, but they had no idea what else to do. After a
little while, without thinking, Bill began to sing to himself
'The Song'. It brought him peace of mind. He wasn't
even aware that the others were listening, but Mr Jenkins
remarked on the beautiful words. So Bill shyly shared with
them how the song had been written and what a change it

had made to their lives. The Jenkinses were very thrilled to hear this, for they were also Christians.

"After all this is over you must tell us more," he said to Bill.

"Theo has told me that you want Tyler to read the Bible to you," remarked Sally. "I bought myself a modern one when I bought one for Theo, but I must admit that I haven't read it yet. If God hears your prayer and brings our boys back safe and sound, I promise I will read it and find out more about him. I used to love going to Sunday school when I was young, but as I grew older I went less and less until I stopped altogether. I have thought about Jesus quite a lot since everything went wrong in my marriage," she added.

Police sirens sounded in the distance, and they all jumped to their feet, running out to the yard.

There seemed to be police everywhere! An officer came over to them.

"We seem to have another crime on our hands," he said, "We have caught a gang trying to rustle your tractor from the top field. They were in the middle of getting it into a truck when we came down the road. Fortunately, we had back-up with us, as we were coming to a serious incident."

"What about our boys? Have they been found?"

"Not as yet, but now these men are duly handcuffed and ready for the cells, every officer I have will be out looking for them."

The policeman's radio bleeped.

"Yes?" he asked. "Any news?"

"We have found the bikes in a hedge further down the road. There is also a locked white van parked nearby. We are breaking into it now. Over and out!"

A few minutes later the good news came through.

"Two boys and one dog all in the back of the van! The boys seem OK, not sure about the dog. Will phone through for ambulance to get the boys checked, and will need a vet, I think."

Bill phoned the castle at once to tell his wife the good news, and asked her to phone gran. The officer then took them to the van where the boys were now wrapped in warm blankets and telling the police their story.

When Bill, Sally and Mr Jenkins arrived, after hugs all round they had to begin again!

Theo and Tyler did have to have quick check ups at the hospital, but apart from a graze where Tyler had fallen when the gate was opened, they were both fine and allowed to go home.

It was late when everyone finally got to bed in their own homes. How thankful they were that nothing worse had happened to the boys! Sally lay in her bed and realised that their prayers had been answered and remembered her promise to God. She quietly told him that she wanted to learn more about him and allow him to be in her life. Then, she too fell into sound asleep. The next morning, in spite of all the excitement, everyone at Syding Castle was awake early. What a blessing there were only a couple of guests who had not realised all the drama that had happened the night before! As soon as he was up, Theo wanted to ring the Jenkins family to find out how Rover was. Paul answered the phone.

"The vet gave him an antidote to the poison and he was sick all over the yard! Tim and Tessa have been hosing it all down. You never saw such a mess! But we don't mind because Rover is fine! We heard all the noise of the police vans, but didn't know that you and Tyler were involved! Thank goodness you are both OK!"

Later that day the police came to take a proper statement from Theo. He took the officer up to his turret room and showed him how he could see almost all the farms in the area, and how he had seen a white van and a truck at Cowleaze farm the time when the tractor had been stolen from there. The police officer was delighted to have this piece of evidence. The gang were not going to be allowed bail, so the boys did not need to be afraid. Not only were they being charged with theft of farm vehicles, but also of kidnapping!

At Honeysuckle cottage, another policeman was not only taking Tyler's statement, but was also apologising profusely to his father for arresting him without any reason other than that he was a gypsy, when the tractor had been stolen from Cowleaze Farm.

Tyler was so happy that for once, his father was no longer under suspicion. He also felt sure that there must be a God who answers prayer, for he had prayed very much in the back of that van!

By the time Monday morning arrived and they were back at school, everyone in the class had heard the story from Paul, Tim and Tessa. They were usually the first at school because their dad brought them straight after milking. Because of all the excitement, Mr Stevens decided that the class should discuss the incident and see what they all could learn from it all. He felt it would help 'debrief' the Jenkins children and the two 'T's'.

Paul Jenkins, the eldest in the family told everyone how he had got to know Tyler when attending the Bible club and also that they realised how nice he was and not at all different, and certainly not untrustworthy just because he was a gypsy! Then Tim, who was usually very shy, also stood up and told everyone that they had been really mean to Theo just because he was clever and had gone to a 'posh' school. He turned to Theo and said, "Sorry Theo, you are really a cool guy!" and the whole class murmured 'sorry' not just to Theo, but also to Tyler.

Theo then put his hand up. "Mr Stevens," he said, "I think I learnt lots of things, but one important lesson was not to rush off and do something without letting my mum know. If I had just taken a few minutes to text or phone her before we began to chase the white van, everyone would have known where we were. When she tried to phone me, I was tied up and couldn't answer."

The class talked about how important this was, especially living in the country as they did and having to get to places on their own. They talked about being responsible.

"How about you, Tyler? Have you anything to add?" Mr Stevens asked.

"Well," said Tyler, standing up and going very red, "don't laugh at me or think I am a sissy, but I think I learnt a bit about God. When my dad kept getting taken down to the police station on suspicion of stealing tractors, I was very mad. Why do people think that all gypsies are bad? Some are bad just like some 'gorgers' are bad; but my dad is not one of those! Anyway, one night my mum was so upset we said a sort of prayer together that the right criminals would be found and dad's name cleared. Also, when we were tied up and gagged in the van on Saturday night, Theo and I didn't know what to do, but Theo managed to get on his knees and closed his eyes, at the same time as trying to tell me to pray. I did! I couldn't speak out loud, but rolled onto my knees, closed my eyes and whispered in my head and prayed hard that someone would find us and also that Rover would be OK. Well, I know it wasn't by accident that we were found and the thieves caught and Rover didn't die. God really did answer, I am sure!"

Everyone in the class was quiet after Tyler's speech, until Mr Stevens spoke.

"You have been brave to tell us that, Tyler. It takes a very brave person to share their beliefs, not a sissy at all. I pray too, and I know God loves to hear and to answer our prayers. He wants to be a father to us and wants us to love him."

Nobody teased Tyler for what he had said, and Theo told him about the night he had prayed and how God had taken away his hate and anger. When it came to Bible club later that week, a couple of their classmates decided to come and see what it was about. Paul, Tim and Tessa shared that they had all become Christians through a Kidszone Club at the church and asked Tyler and Theo if they wanted to join the club too.

"That sounds like a good idea," said Tyler, and Theo agreed. Although the experience of being kidnapped had been very scary in many ways, it created a bond between the three families. The parents began to meet together to learn more from the Bible and pray together. It became the talk of the village for a while that the supposedly rich lady in the castle and the gypsies had become friends, and they were all friends with the Jenkins family who had farmed in the area for generations.

Once gran was stronger, she began to look after little
Sunshine so that Betty was able to go and help Sally at the
castle with the running of the B&B business. Farmer Jenkins
and Bill both helped out when repair jobs were needed
in the house and outhouses, and all the families enjoyed
the swimming pool and the games room. As life became
easier, Sally felt as if a huge weight had been lifted off her
shoulders.

Chapter Fourteen

The summer term was going so quickly! Theo didn't want it to end. Even though he had hated the village school when he first had to move there, now he loved it so much he wasn't looking forward to leaving and going to senior school!

He was enjoying being the captain of the cricket team and a match had been arranged for them to play against their parents. The Saturday of the match was perfect, warm and sunny, with very little breeze. Ten boys and one girl had been chosen for the team and they had been practising hard. Several of the children had their fathers playing in the parents' team, but even though Theo knew his dad would have been a star player, he no longer felt angry that he had left them; just a little sad. Both Farmer Jenkins and Bill were in the team. The parents won the toss and put the school team into bat. Theo was the opening batsman and Laura, the only girl player, was number two. Between them they did well, Laura scoring 31 and Theo managing 72 before he was bowled out. In all, the school team did very well reaching a total score of 210. They had a tea break with lovely food made by some of the mothers, and Mr Stevens said how proud he was of their performance.

When the parents' team went into bat, Tyler took the first over, since he was the best bowler. He got his own dad out for a duck! Everyone thought that was extremely funny! Some of the parents had not played for years, but one or two were in the village cricket team and put up a very good fight. In the end, the parents won by a wicket and ten runs, but it had been great fun and everyone declared it should be a regular feature on the school calendar and the cricket club should continue!

Just before term ended, years five and six planned a trip to Brownsea Island. Tyler was so excited because Mr Stevens had told them they might see red squirrels there! It was a two-day trip. Everyone had to get to school by 7 a.m. for an early start. The coach was waiting for them, and they headed to Poole Quay to catch the ferry. That in itself was quite exciting. Some of the children had never been on a boat, but the sea was calm and no one felt sick. Then they landed on the island and made their way to a camp site. The children were allocated a tent where they were to sleep and Theo, Tyler and Paul were all in the same one along with a boy whose name was Simon. Once they were settled they had some time to explore their surroundings before lunch. One of the school dinner ladies and her friend had come to do the cooking. They ate outside as the weather was lovely. It reminded Theo of eating outside at Tyler's house, and everything tasted so much nicer!

In the afternoon they went to the activity centre and an instructor helped them to learn archery or to build a den. Theo and Tyler both wanted to make a den. They decided in the summer holidays they could build their own den in the woods. Paul and Simon both had archery lessons. It was all such fun and the afternoon passed so quickly! While the cooks made supper Mr Stevens and another teacher took the class down to the beach, where they were able to play on the shore and also eat ice cream!

A fire had been lit on the camp site and sausages and jacket potatoes cooked over it. The children sat on logs around it and after they had eaten they sang 'camp fire songs'. The two 'T's' didn't want it to end, but due to the early start to the day, everyone soon felt very sleepy. Once they climbed in their sleeping bags, it wasn't long before they were all sound asleep.

They woke early next morning to hear birds singing. As soon as breakfast was over the class was divided into small groups. Each group had a warden who was going to take them trekking and look for wildlife. Many of the things he told them, the two 'T's' already knew, but they didn't mind. Tyler was just praying that he might see a red squirrel! They saw several interesting insects then suddenly, they came across a herd of sika deer. The children were very quiet as they watched the beautiful animals. Some of them had cameras and were able to take photos. They had a picnic lunch sitting in a clearing in the trees, and as they were eating, Theo saw a red squirrel. Excitedly, he poked Tyler and pointed. The squirrel almost seemed to pose for them, standing on its hind legs and looking directly at them. The warden who had also seen it gathered the children together so they could see too. Tyler was thrilled to bits! It was just as beautiful as his dad had told him! The little ears pointed upwards and the red coloured fur was exquisite! Paul was one of the photographers and he took several shots before the squirrel scampered up a tree and out of their sight. He promised he would get prints for Tyler and Theo.

Later that afternoon the warden took them on a walk exploring the island's wartime history, and this pleased Paul very much. They had been studying the Second World War in history, and he had been very interested as his grandfather had been in the navy and worked on submarines during that time.

They all had to be back at the camp site by five o'clock, in order to have some tea, tidy up and catch the ferry back to the mainland. Nobody wanted to go home! Once back in Poole they found the coach was waiting for them and climbed aboard. Mr Stevens told them how Enid Blyton had been inspired by the island and called it 'Whispering Island' in her Famous Five books. Then they began to sing 'camp fire songs' again and just about managed to keep awake for the rest of the journey! It had been a fantastic treat. Theo was so pleased, not only had Tyler seen the red squirrel, but also, no one had been horrid to either of them. They both felt accepted by their class mates. It made him hope that they would fit in to the senior school next term. He wasn't much looking forward to the change, but he knew that Jesus would be with him and help him. He hoped there would be a Bible club there also and made a mental note to ask Seb and Flick about it.

Chapter Fifteen

The end of term came so quickly! At the leavers' service in the village church, Tyler had a big surprise. The headmaster called him out and presented him with a cup for the pupil who had made the greatest improvement throughout the year! His parents were sitting with Theo's mum and Mr and Mrs Jenkins. They all beamed with delight! He was presented with a Bible just like Theo's, and he was so pleased and proud. From being almost unable to read at the start of the school year he could now read fluently, and had achieved his ambition of being able to read the Bible to his parents!

At the end of his talk, the Vicar made an announcement. As so many of the village children were not able to go away for a holiday because it was such a busy time on the farms and for people who ran hotels and bed and breakfast etc, he had asked a team of students to come and run a holiday club for a week. He invited all the children to come and bring their brothers and sisters who were aged between five and thirteen. He made it sound like fun, and Theo certainly thought he would like to attend and was sure his friends would, too.

All of year six seemed sad to leave the village school, but at least most of them would go to the comprehensive in Dorchester, so they would still be together. Meanwhile, there were six weeks of holiday! Tyler, Theo and the Jenkins children had made lots of plans. They would have a lot of fun!

A week or so after school finished the fair arrived! It came every year for three days and set up on the village green. Tyler was so excited as many of his gypsy relatives came with their rides and stalls. Honeysuckle Cottage was always full as people came to see them and gran, who was now well and back in her vardo. When the fair closed at night all the extended family gathered around the camp fire and sang and danced. Bill played his violin and he and Betty sang together. It was magical! No one minded how late it was and all the children were allowed to stay up. Tales would be told around the camp fire, sometimes in the Romany language, sometimes in English. One night, Bill and Betty sang 'The Song' together. The beautiful tune and words about Jesus made all the listeners very quiet. It was so special! Then, Bill began to tell his family the story of 'The Song' and how it had changed their lives so that they had become Christians, followers of Jesus. It was as if a heavenly peace had fallen on everyone, for nobody made fun of Bill and Betty. When his father had finished, something stirred in Tyler and he began to speak.

"I was very upset when this happened to my mum and dad," he explained, at first shyly, then more boldly, "I didn't understand why our lives had changed so much and why we weren't travelling and mum had given up telling fortunes, but throughout this year my life has changed too. I found I could speak to God and he listened and things happened. I have a great friend called Theo and he helped me and we read the Bible together. Both of us now love Jesus. Now I understand that I can be Romany and also a Christian and am no longer confused."

When Tyler finished, some of his relatives clapped, and suddenly he felt very shy again, but he was glad he had told them his story.

Almost everyone in the village went to the fair. Theo, Tyler and Paul loved the coconut shy and won so many! There was an archery stall, too, and Paul did very well at that after his lessons on Brownsea Island. Little Sunshine spent most of her time being taken on the roundabout by various relatives or by Felicity who was now like a big sister to her!

As well as the gypsy rides and stalls many local people had stalls with home made produce or crafts. Tyler and his dad had a stall with carvings; gran had some soaps and lotions which she made from herbs; Mrs Jenkins had a wonderful stall full of her delicious home-made cakes and biscuits. There was candy floss and ice creams and all sorts of other food. There was fun for however young or old you were!

At the end of the three days Tyler and his family said goodbye to all their relatives and Romany friends. Suddenly the village was quiet again! The boys helped clear up any litter and the village green soon looked as it always did. That was as well because the school cricket club had decided to meet there each week and keep playing through the holidays.

Tyler and Theo built their den in the woods. It really was a good den and they wanted to sleep out one night. At first their parents refused, but then they agreed, so long as Bill could bring a tent and sleep near them.

They made a camp fire and cooked sausages, which got a bit burnt, but were very tasty. When it became dark, Bill took them on a badger hunt on into the night! They first looked for spoor and then for hairs left on tree trunks that had become 'scratching posts' near the sets. Badgers are very shy creatures so they had to be very quiet, but they did see a large male with a smaller badger, presumably his mate and three cubs. It was enchanting! It was very late when they crept into their sleeping bags. It was also very late when they woke up the next morning to find the sun streaming into their den and all the birds singing! Tyler's dad already had breakfast cooking for them. Following that they went to the cottage and had a wash! It had been such fun they asked if they could do it again!

Up at the castle business was good. There were many visitors and all the children had to help their mum, but Betty came each day to help out and life was easier for all of them. The weather was still fine and the children made good use of the swimming pool. Often Paul, Tim and Tessa joined them. In the days when their dad had lived at home the children had ponies. Felicity, in particular, really missed her pony. She occasionally managed to go to a riding school for a lesson, but it cost too much to go very often. One day Betty had a good idea. Her mother's pony, Sparks, was not getting enough exercise now that he no longer pulled the vardo. He had also grazed almost every bit of grass near the cottage. She wondered if Sparks could come to the castle for Flick to look after him, and suggested it to Sally.

"What a wonderful idea!" said Theo's mum, "Flick would be so happy to have a pony to care for again!"

When Felicity was asked if she would look after Sparks, she whooped in delight!

"Can I go and get a stable ready now?" she asked her mum. "I will take the best care of him!"

Later that day Sparks came to his new home. Not only did Felicity take wonderful care of him, but all the children were able to ride him, using all sorts of old riding gear which had been found after the loft had been searched. Soon Sparks was fit once more.

Theo's oldest sister Penny, rarely played with them. She was devoted to her music and practised the piano as much as she could in her spare time. Not long before term ended, she had been entered for her grade eight exam and it was during the holiday that she received the news that she had passed with distinction and even better, had been given a scholarship in a music school in Manchester.

Everyone was thrilled for her, but Sally was secretly worried about whether she could afford to let her go. A scholarship was one thing, but kitting her daughter out and paying for her to be in the National Youth Orchestra was quite another, plus, how would she manage without her help at the castle?

One morning, she shared her worries with Betty.

"I can't not let her have this chance. It's all she ever dreamed of! I feel so angry at my ex-husband. He should be supporting and helping us! What can I do?" Tears began to well up in her eyes.

"There is one thing we know we can do," answered her friend. "Let's pray about it."

So quietly they just told God about the problem and asked for his help.

Chapter Sixteen

A few days later, they were busy cleaning the bedrooms after the guests had gone when the doorbell rang. On the doorstep was the vicar of Much Syding Church. The mothers had seen him at the school leavers' service but had not met him before. He introduced himself and asked if he could come in for a chat, as he had a request to make. Sally made them all coffee and they sat around the kitchen table.

"I do hope you don't mind me calling," the vicar said, "Mr Stevens thought you might be able to help. We are having a holiday club, as you know, the last week in August. I just wondered if one afternoon we might be able to use your swimming pool and games room for the children. The church will pay you for the use, and one of the students leading the club is a trained life guard, so there would be no safety issue. The weather isn't always very good at the end of August, and to have an indoor activity would be so helpful. Don't feel you have to give me an answer at once, but if you could think it over, I would be very grateful."

"I don't really need to think it over," replied Theo's mum. "I am very happy for you to use it any time you wish, so long as the children are supervised. You can use the grounds too as long as adults make sure they are treated with respect. There are several barns and outhouses where you could have activities. "That is wonderful," the vicar said. "When we have finalised the programme I'll ring and fix a date. I wasn't sure how you would feel about children coming here. I really want to bring young people into our church family."

"My son is very keen to come to the club, but a bit afraid that gypsies won't be welcome," said Betty. "We are Christians too, but so many people are suspicious of gypsies we decided not to come to church. Before we moved here we did try, but it was a disaster," she added.

The vicar was horrified. "I am so sad to hear you say that! You will always be welcome at our church. The wonderful thing about the church, is that it is all inclusive, no matter what age, class, race or creed. It is meant to be a family that crosses all these barriers! You make sure your son comes along to the club, and I would love to see you at church any time you can come!"

Later on that day the vicar phoned to make arrangements. Theo's mum really didn't want payment for use of the premises, but he insisted. As he said, he would feel happy to ask for use of the premises for other gatherings like a barn dance at harvest, if she accepted the payment.

Suddenly, Sally realised that God was answering her prayer and providing some extra income to send Penny to the music school. It wasn't a lot, but every little helped and somehow she realised she could trust the Lord to provide it all.

That evening after supper, Sally told the children she wanted to talk to them. Once the chickens were safely in their coop and the garden watered, they gathered for a family conference.

The children learnt about the vicar's visit and were happy to share the games room and pool and also their mother told them about her prayer for more money and how quickly it had been answered. "I am sure," she said, "that God will provide all that Penny needs for her new school and also the things Theo needs to start at seniors. Your dad may not provide for you, but you have a heavenly Father who will. I hope that one day you will all trust him to be your Father as I am learning to do; he will never go away and let you down."

Penny was so excited! She had thought she would not be able to take up her scholarship.

"But will you manage here at home?" she asked her Mum.

"I am sure I will. With Betty's help and with so many guests booked in this summer I can afford to pay her. So off you go and accept the scholarship!"

Penny didn't need telling twice. She ran to the computer to write her letter! The next few days were wet and windy. Tyler came over and the two 'T's' spent time up in the turret. They were looking at the map which they had made of the castle grounds, and there was one place in the kitchen garden where the metal detector had made a tremendous noise. Theo had found it hard to keep it in his hands! They decided to ask if they could dig and find what was there.

After lunch Theo asked his mum and she agreed they could dig so long as it wasn't too big a hole. He and Tyler put on their wellies and found some spades in the outhouse. Even though it had rained for some days the ground was still quite hard. Eventually, Tyler came across a wooden box. The boys couldn't wait to get it up and open it! When they did, inside were six spoons, all rather black and uninteresting. The boys were disappointed, but at least had something to show for all their digging. They filled in the hole as they had promised and took the box of spoons into the kitchen.

"This is what we found," Theo showed his mum the old box of black spoons.

"Wow!" she said as she looked at them. "I think they are silver." She turned one spoon over and found some letters and symbols. "I will try and clean them and we can take them to the auction rooms in Dorchester. They will know what the marks mean."

The next afternoon she took the boys to Dorchester where they were able to have someone look at the spoons. The man became very excited.

"I think you have a real find here! This is fine Georgian silver." He put a special magnifying glass into his eye and peered at the marks. "Yes, not a doubt! A complete set and made by the best maker!" He turned and smiled at the boys. "Quite a treasure you have found in your garden!"

"And we thought they were useless black old spoons!" remarked Tyler. "I wonder who hid them there!"

"I guess someone stole them and hoped to dig them up at a later date when all the hue and cry stopped. It must have been a long time ago though, because of the state of both the box and the spoons."

After some discussion it was agreed that they would be cleaned properly and sold at auction in September.

On the way home Theo became excited. "God really is answering our prayers! I am so glad we know about him now! It's like you said Mum, we must trust him to provide for us, and he is!"

The boys were so excited that they went up to Castle View farm to share the news with the Jenkins family. The Jenkins said they had better come there with the metal detector!

It was the last week of August and the holiday club arrived. Theo, Tyler, Paul, Tim and Tessa had all signed up along with other friends from school. At first the twins turned up their noses and said they were too old and not interested, but by the Wednesday they too had come to join in the fun and games. They went trekking in the woods, making camp fires; did craft and played all sorts of games, as well as having Bible times when they learnt more about Jesus. Sometimes they acted things out and Felicity really enjoyed that as she had ambitions to become an actress!

On the Friday the club went to the castle for the afternoon. The children were proud and pleased when everyone loved their home. It was a great success. Even Sparks the pony got lots of attention, and Felicity helped some of the younger children to have rides. Theo and Tyler's mothers provided refreshments in the barn, and they ended up singing some of the new songs they had learnt through the week. A particular favourite was, "Jesus is with me wherever I go, Jesus is with me I know."

The two 'T's' were feeling quite apprehensive about starting the following week at their new school and somehow singing the song helped them to feel more confident about the huge changes that were about to happen. They talked about the past year and how they had hated starting at the village school, but what a wonderful year it had turned out to be! They were best friends and had also made lots of other friends, but more wonderful than all that: they had come to know Jesus as their Friend, too!

Coming soon in the Syding Adventures

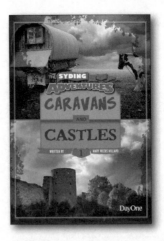

CARAVANS AND CASTLES (1)

Mary Weeks Millard

ISBN 978-1-84625-364-5

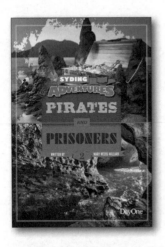

PIRATES AND PRISONERS (2)

Mary Weeks Millard

ISBN 978-1-84625-365-2

SUNSHINE AND SNOWSTORMS (3)

Mary Weeks Millard

ISBN 978-1-84625-366-9

ROMANS AND RANSOMS (4)

Mary Weeks Millard

ISBN 978-1-84625-367-6

LIVE WIRES AND LOBSTER POTS (5)

Mary Weeks Millard

ISBN 978-1-84625-368-3

VIKINGS AND VISITORS (6)

Mary Weeks Millard

ISBN 978-1-84625-369-0

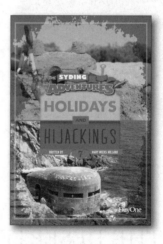

HOLIDAYS AND HIJACKINGS (7)

Mary Weeks Millard

ISBN 978-1-84625-370-6

If you enjoyed these you might like the following books by Mary Weeks Millard

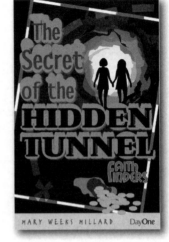

THE SECRET OF THE HIDDEN TUNNEL

Mary Weeks Millard

ISBN 978-1-84625-334-8

NEVER GIVE UP ON YOUR DREAMS

Mary Weeks Millard

ISBN 978-1-84625-271-6

THE MYSTERY OF THE DESERTED HOUSE

Mary Weeks Millard

ISBN 978 1 84625 272 3

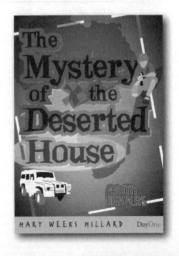